POWERPLAY

NORTHBROOK HOCKEY ELITE

Heather B. Moore
Sophia Summers
Rebecca Connolly

POWERPLAY

NORTHBROOK HOCKEY ELITE

Interior design by Cora Johnson
Edited by Kelsey Down and Lorie Humpherys
Cover design by Rachael Anderson
Cover image credit: Deposit Photos #193361580
Published by Mirror Press, LLC

ISBN: 978-1-947152-83-0

POWERPLAY

He's ready to quit his pro hockey career. She's doing everything to keep her career afloat. And neither of them has time for distractions.

Jax Emerson, legendary forward for the Chicago Flyers, is ready to throw it all away when he uncovers the truth behind his NHL contract. The last thing he needs is more media attention, or his father to get involved in his contract, or a beautiful woman apologizing once again for an accident.

Meg Bailey didn't think her life could get any worse, until it does. Time is running out before her business will be forced to close. When Jax Emerson offers a solution, she knows that by accepting his help, she might be getting in too deep. And deep is not a place her heart is prepared to go.

ONE

AT SIX FOOT five, Jax Emerson should be used to living in a world of tiny people. Either that, or those he interviewed with should recognize that he was taller and broader than average and he wouldn't fit into a mini office chair behind a desk that crowded his knees.

Case in point. He was currently mic'd up, sitting next to the top sports newscaster in Chicago, wedged into a chair that was likely made for a five-foot-two human, and trying to avoid answering any personal questions. Such was the world of media and pro sports. When did they ever get to talk about the game—especially last night's, when Jax had played the best game of his career? Scoring three points in the first period and setting a team record for the Chicago Flyers.

Of course, the Seattle Blacks got pretty wise after that and had double-teamed Jax. He hadn't minded. He'd already scored the points, and the Blacks never recovered fully. The Flyers had won, three to one.

"As the only Chicago native on the team," Bud Roseman said, adjusting his horn-rimmed glasses, "you sure have some loyal fans. They went crazy over your stellar first-period performance."

Finally. "Thank you, sir," Jax murmured.

Who would ever name their kid Bud? Jax wondered as the bright lights of the news-station room felt like they were burning a hole into his forehead. Was Bud short for Buddy, or was it some childhood nickname that never could be shaken off? Now, *Jax* was a more respectable nickname, and it made sense for someone named Jackson.

"But what the fans would be really crazy to know is who Jax Emerson, the top hockey forward in all of Chicago, is dating?" Roseman said with a chuckle.

Jax blinked. Then he looked for that water bottle a pretty blond had set on the desk just before the cameras started rolling. Locating it, he twisted off the top and took a long swallow. Yep. He was stalling.

His agent, Scott, had warned Jax about this, but he'd laughed it off. Roseman was a professional, right? Perhaps the question had been innocent, but it bothered him all the same. Scott had said that the Flyers' owners wanted the team to attend more fundraisers and social events now that they were actually winning this season. The hockey team owners wanted to capitalize on it, sell more tickets, bring on more sponsors, fill the depleted coffers.

"Bring your family," Scott had said, "your parents."

"No one else is bringing their parents," Jax had countered.

"Then bring a date," Scott had continued. "Since you don't have a girlfriend or a wife like most of the other players. Get the Lone Wolf trending again."

No. Jax had no girlfriend or wife. And yes, he'd been called the Lone Wolf on Twitter, and he supposed it fit. All potential for any decent relationship with a woman had ended in disaster over a year ago. And Jax had his own dad to thank. There was a good reason Jax didn't date, casually or otherwise.

Number one reason, his father. Number two reason, his father. The man would do anything, and had done everything, to control Jax's life. Last year, Jax had found out that his father had been bribing Lacy, his now ex-girlfriend.

She'd been *paid* to date him. Paid to be the perfect girlfriend. Paid to look good for the media, to say the right things, to pretend she was in love with him. She'd acted her part so well that he'd thought he'd fallen in love with her too.

On the night he was going to propose, he overheard her on the phone with his dad. Negotiating her next payout.

The year-old memory sat like a sour lemon in his throat. Jax picked up the water bottle again. He still hadn't answered Bud Roseman's question. Perhaps he wouldn't. Perhaps he'd walk out of the Channel KTMX news station right now. Or was it KTNX?

But Bud Roseman wasn't the top sportscaster for nothing. "While Jax Emerson keeps hydrated and thinks about his answer, we'll go to a quick commercial break. Stay tuned, folks, for the next segment of our interview, when things get personal with Chicago's number one hockey player."

A commercial played on the surrounding screens, and Jax stood.

Bud popped to his feet. "Can I get you something, Mr. Emerson?"

Jax unclipped the mic from the button-down shirt his agent had also insisted he wear. Dressy clothes reminded Jax of his dad, so he avoided wearing anything upgraded from a T-shirt and jeans whenever possible.

"Thanks for having me, sir," Jax said. "But our interview is over." He looked the man right in the eyes—brown eyes below thick brows. "You overstepped your bounds. I was prepared to talk hockey."

Bud's mouth opened, then closed. His brows nearly connected, forming a rather impressive unibrow.

3

"Have a nice day." Jax stepped away from the desk, then nodded to the cameramen, who looked like they'd just watched a car do a double flip in midair.

Perhaps Bud Roseman called after Jax, but he didn't really know, because he was out the door before anyone else could react or try to stop him. Not that they could, at least physically. Jax wasn't 240 pounds of muscle because he edited books for a living. As the left wing forward for the Chicago Flyers, he was known for scoring on a powerplay. And he'd just made a decision that would probably anger his agent, and his father if he caught wind as well.

As he headed down the emergency stairwell of the news building, Jax pulled up Scott's number.

His agent answered with, "What's wrong? Aren't you in the middle of an interview? I just saw the commercial break."

Jax paused in the stairwell, somewhere between the second and first floor of the building. In careful tones, he explained what had happened.

Scott was silent for so long that Jax wondered if the stairwell had cruddy reception. Had Scott heard a word that Jax said?

"Fine." Scott finally cleared his throat. "You walked out of an interview. Maybe we can say you were sick or had a migraine or something. You did take some hard hits last night."

"No excuses," Jax said. "I told Roseman where he crossed the line. As far as I'm concerned, I've done everyone in pro hockey a favor."

Scott blew out a breath. "Here's the thing, Jax. You're already known as a hothead, but the media are our friends right now. Keep your temper on the ice. Off of it, think of something besides your own ego."

The words burned in Jax's chest. "I have every right not to answer questions about my personal life."

"Would it have hurt you to just say, *No, I'm not dating anyone right now?*"

Jax wrapped one hand around the metal railing of the stairwell. "It's the principal of the matter."

"What are you going to tell your dad?"

Jax's brows popped up at this. "What does my dad have to do with me walking out on an interview?"

"Nothing," Scott was quick to say. "Just that you're representing your family in all of this too. You know, the Emerson name."

Jax scoffed. "Just because my dad owns half the businesses in Chicago doesn't mean he gets a say in my career."

The pause was a couple of seconds too long before Scott said, "Well, let's just hope this stays on the down-low. Commercial's over; I'll see how well Roseman recovers."

But Jax was no longer thinking of the botched interview. His stomach had knotted tighter than a noose. "Turn off your TV," he growled. "Now."

"What the h—"

"Tell me now why you think it will be *my dad's* concern if I walk out on an interview."

Something clattered in the background.

"Answer me now," Jax ground out. "And if I find out you're holding anything back, you're fired."

There was no way Jax could have prepared himself for what Scott said next. It was a good thing he was alone and had a stair to sit on.

"Your, uh, dad put money into the Flyers," Scott said, his normally confident tone hesitant.

Okay. This wasn't anything to stress over. His dad donated to a lot of things, sponsored everything from Boy Scouts to women's shelters. Mostly to put forward a good public image. Had nothing to do with helping people. Oh, and the tax write-off. "How much are we talking about?"

Jax expected Scott to come back with maybe ten or fifteen grand.

"The amount of your contract."

Everything inside of Jax went still. Then the blood rushed to his ears. "My contract?" he asked. "Three million a year?"

"Yes." Scott's voice sounded like he was choking, and perhaps he was.

Jax dropped his phone. It clattered onto the next step below, then rotated in some sort of slow-motion spin. A fine crack snaked across the screen.

Scott's voice continued coming from the phone, but it sounded tinny, far away.

Jax dropped his head into his hands and squeezed his eyes shut.

His entire pro hockey career had been a farce. His father had bribed and paid for the Flyers to offer him. Yeah, Jax's dad had paid his club fees back when he played with Northbrook Hockey Elite during high school. He'd even sponsored fees for other promising players who struggled financially. But this . . . this was different.

Scott's voice sounded through the phone. Just words. Nothing made sense anymore.

Jax snatched the phone from the step and hit END on the call. Then he turned the thing completely off and pocketed it. He jogged down the rest of the steps to the ground floor. He slammed a palm against the exit door and strode into the cold wind of the Chicago December day.

He was done. More than done with his father interfering. Maybe Jax would quit the team, teach his dad a lesson. Maybe he'd do a trade. Contract or no contract, Jax would put himself on the market. Injuries happened all the time, and there would be openings. He ignored the doubt about his ability at the edge of his mind—his dad might have bought his contract, but Jax was still an impact player.

Last night had proved it. His entire eight-year pro career had proved it.

Maybe it was time to fire his agent. Then Scott would really have something to worry about, like his own paycheck.

Whatever happened, Jax needed to clear his head. He wasn't sure where he was going or what he'd do when he got there. Maybe he'd stay off the grid for a few days. Rent a cabin.

Without looking left or right, Jax walked, ignoring the fact that the icy wind cut through his dress shirt and slacks, ignoring the flashes of recognition as people pointed him out on the street. He even ignored the traffic light.

But he didn't mean to step in front of an oncoming car.

And the last thing he heard was the squeal of brakes, or maybe it was the scream of a woman? He didn't have time to figure it out, because he was flying through the air, then he landed on something hard and cold and wet.

And his vision went completely black.

TWO

"I DIDN'T SEE him," Meghan Bailey said into her phone. "I swear I didn't see him. One second no one was there, the next he was in front of me."

"Ma'am," the 911 dispatcher said. "Remain calm and tell me if he's breathing."

"I don't know," Meg said. "He's just lying there."

"Ma'am"—the calm voice spoke again—"feel the pulse on his neck."

Sirens wailed in the distance, and the sound jolted through her like a bullet had pierced her chest. The sirens were a result of *her*. Hitting a man with her car.

Meg blinked back her tears because everything was blurry now.

"Do you feel a pulse?" the dispatcher asked.

"I'm doing it now." Meg knelt beside the man, who was lying so still that it took her breath away. Could she really touch a dead man?

The sirens were getting closer, and a crowd had gathered at the sidewalk, but no one was coming into the street to help.

"Is anyone a doctor?" she yelled in a frantic voice. "Or a nurse? Anyone?"

"Ma'am?"

"I'm trying," she said into the phone. "I don't know if I can touch him."

"Ma'am, check if he has a pulse. Administering CPR might be necessary, and it can save his life before the ambulance gets there."

Meg wanted to throw up. It was up to her, then. She placed two fingers on the man's neck. "He's alive," she whispered.

The dispatcher said something else, but the sirens were too loud for Meg to understand the woman's words.

Meg didn't move, didn't lift her fingers from the man's warm neck and the steady thumping of his pulse.

His eyes were closed, and his eyelashes were so very still. His hair was a dark auburn brown, although there was some copper color in his beard. He'd probably been a redhead as a kid, with a sweet redheaded mother and a fun, adventurous father. Maybe this man had a wife who was wondering why her husband wasn't texting her back. His wife was most certainly beautiful, the kind of woman who went to the spa weekly. For this man was beautiful too. And wealthy.

His designer clothing and expensive watch were a testament to that. If anyone knew clothing, Meg did. As the owner of Meg's Loft, she spent her days running the clothing boutique and bringing in eclectic designer clothing. Never major designers or big-box brands, only unique clothing.

The sirens were louder now, crowding out all thought. Her chest tightened, and she couldn't take a full breath. *Relax, Meg,* she told herself, but nothing on her body was relaxed. She didn't need anyone to tell her that she was in shock.

The sirens finally cut off, and someone grasped her arm and pulled her back. "Give us room, ma'am," a man's voice said.

Help. Help was here. The man was breathing, and the paramedics would help him.

She rose to her feet, although her legs felt like water.

The paramedics checked the man's pulse, then someone said, "One, two, three," and the man was hefted onto a gurney. His feet dangled off the too-short gurney. Didn't they have gurneys for taller people?

Was it something she should have mentioned to the dispatcher? *Can you send an extra-long gurney?*

Meg was hysterical; that was what was going on. No, she wasn't screaming or crying, but her entire body had frozen. She watched as the man was loaded into the back of the ambulance, with its flashing lights. Her heart splintered as the sirens blared again and the ambulance pulled away.

She could have killed a man. She still might have.

"Ma'am, please move out of the road."

Meg turned to see a police officer with a pocked face and graying hair. "I need to follow the ambulance," she said in a hoarse voice. "I need to see how he's doing."

The officer frowned. "Let the doctors do their job. I need a statement from you."

Meg brought a hand to her mouth. Inhaled. Exhaled. "Of course."

"Come with me," the officer said.

Meg answered all of his questions to the best of her ability, and when the officer was done, she was surprised she was still standing, still breathing, still living. Did others look at her and think she was normal? She felt far from normal. She'd never be the same again.

Because the officer was telling her about a court appearance she might have to make, depending on the statement made by the guy she hit.

Meg could scarcely take it all in. "Which hospital did he go to?" she blurted out.

"Northwestern Memorial is the closest one," the officer said. "But, ma'am, I don't think it's a good idea for you to show up there. The family might call security."

Meg stepped back. "I have to . . . I have to know . . ."

She turned from the officer, who merely watched her go. The front bumper of her car had fared much better than the man, and she climbed into the car. Perhaps she shouldn't be driving, but she couldn't very well leave her car here.

Gripping the steering wheel with both hands, she drove to the hospital. Somehow she made it to visitor's parking and managed to pull in straight. Then she locked her car and headed into the main lobby.

The bright fluorescent lights buzzed above her, making her realize that the headache she'd had since that morning was now piercing. Her gaze zeroed in on the information desk, and she walked to it, eyeing the twenty-something girl with dark-pink lips working behind the counter. What were the chances of her giving Meg the room number of a man she didn't even know the name of?

Before Meg could say a word, the front doors of the hospital slid open.

"Where is he?" a man said into his phone. He strode toward the information desk, his brows like angry slashes across his forehead. "What do you mean, you don't know? I thought you talked to the cops."

The lobby beyond the information desk quieted as those sitting in chairs looked in the direction of the man on the phone.

"All right," the man said, his voice less fierce now and more resigned as he stopped in front of the information desk. He loosened his tie. "If you're sure it's Northwestern Memorial, then I'm here now. Just get here as fast as you can."

Meg, as unobtrusively as she could, edged away. She'd

wait until this man was helped before she inquired with her question.

The man hung up, and without a glance at Meg, he gazed at the receptionist. "I need the room number of Jackson Emerson. He was brought in about an hour ago. Some bimbo hit him with a car. Unbelievable."

Kudos to the young woman behind the counter, who didn't seem fazed by the harsh words. She merely typed a few things into her computer, then looked up. "Relation?"

The man straightened. "I'm his father."

"I need to see your ID, please."

He huffed but in a smooth motion pulled his wallet from the inside of his suit coat pocket. Then he slid his ID across the counter.

"Very well, Mr. Emerson," the woman said. "Your son is in room 208."

He nodded and was already on the phone before he stepped away from the information desk. "Jax is in room 208. Meet me there." He clicked off his phone and walked toward the elevators.

Meg discovered she was gripping the edge of the information desk. Not just because she'd nearly come face-to-face with the father of the man she'd hit with a car. But because the man she'd hit was Jax Emerson. Star forward of the Chicago Flyers.

She hadn't recognized him ... well, out of context she wasn't surprised, and he hadn't been wearing pads, a uniform, and a helmet. And his eyes had been closed—those intense eyes that stared into the camera, right through the television screen, when he was being interviewed off the ice.

Breathe, Meg.

208. Room 208.

She turned from the information desk and found a lobby

chair to sit in. There was no way she'd go to his hospital room when he had family there. Besides, she was pretty sure his dad was the last person she wanted to talk to right now.

The hospital door swooshed open, and a man strode in. Another expensive-looking man. This one wore a short goatee and a blazer over a pinstriped shirt. He strode past the information desk, straight to the elevators.

A member of the Emerson family?

Meg's pulse hadn't slowed down, and she knew it wouldn't until she found out Jax Emerson's prognosis. This entire week had been pretty lousy, and today had been the pinnacle of that lousiness when she'd gotten the final spreadsheets from her accountant and found out that she had maybe six weeks before she'd have to close down Meg's Loft. With the rent increase she'd been notified of last week, she had known she'd be cutting things really close. Turned out, it was too close.

Meg would have to move her shop to online exclusive, which meant she could still eat and pay expenses but not do what she loved the most: spend her days in a shop, talking fashion and clothing with customers, handling the fabrics, and arranging displays. Sales might be her bread and butter, but her passion was simply the clothing itself.

Meg closed her eyes against the bright fluorescent lights, against the people coming and going, against the ringing phone at the information desk. When her stomach rumbled, she knew it was because she hadn't eaten for hours. How long would Jax's father be at the hospital? The rest of the day? All night?

The hospital doors opened again, and several men walked in. Everyone in the lobby stared. These were not regular men. They were the size of mountains, and Meg's sinking heart told her that they were the pro hockey teammates of Jax Emerson.

She felt the blood drain from her face. How serious were Jax's injuries? And how could she find out?

Her stomach rumbled again, but there was no way Meg could eat.

The television in the lobby had been playing some mundane sitcom, but now a news flash came onto the screen: *Breaking news! Jax Emerson, star player of pro hockey team the Chicago Flyers, was badly injured earlier today when he was hit by a car while crossing the street . . .*

Meg stared in horror at the female reporter. Behind her was the hospital's emergency entrance sign. The media was at the hospital, and Jax Emerson was seriously injured.

THREE

"I NEED THIS out," Jax said, pushing up on his elbows. He was hooked up to some machine with various tubes and wires, none of them necessary.

"Please lie back down, sir," the nurse said, a woman who reminded him of a prison warden, from her iron-gray hair to her no-nonsense blue eyes.

"I'm fine," he said. "I heard the doctor."

Nurse Prim set her hands on her hips. Her name wasn't really Prim, but it fit her better than what her nametag said: *Sonnie.*

"The doctor wants you kept overnight for observation," she said. "Then plenty of rest at home and a follow-up in seven days, with more X-rays."

Jax hid a groan as he shifted to a sitting position. Yeah, he ached, and yeah, things were throbbing, but nothing was broken, torn, or sprained. No concussion either, which was a minor miracle. Only a bit of road rash on his back and shoulder and a deep bruise on his left hip. Something that wouldn't get in the way of anything. Like he had said, he was fine.

The doctor was being overcautious, what with Jax's

father, coach, and assistant coach all breathing down his neck. Of course the doctor was going to recommend a very thorough follow-up. "If nothing's broken now, then nothing's going to show up on an X-ray in another week. Unless I get hit by a car again." The humor went right past Nurse Prim. Not even a hint of a smile.

Jax swung his legs over the bed, slowly because of his hip. He'd refused strong pain medication because he fully intended to leave the hospital tonight. Discharged or not. The droning television in the corner told him that the media had been outside the hospital earlier that day, and the last thing he intended to do was another interview. One interview in a day had been plenty.

Besides, the newscasters had had a field day, from reporting all kinds of injuries, like dislocated limbs and a serious concussion, to informing the greater population of Chicago that Jax Emerson would be out for the rest of the season.

Hell. That was the farthest thing from the truth as possible. Unless things went horribly south with his conversation with his dad about his contract, because he intended to confront his coach as well.

Jax set his feet upon the cold ground. It was after midnight, the perfect time to escape the hospital without the media hounding him. Now, where was his phone?

"Sir," Nurse Prim said, "I'll need to get the doctor if you insist on getting up. His orders were very specific."

"I'm fine," he said, although the room had begun to tilt. He waited a moment, then gripped the railing of the bed as he stood . . . just in case. The dizziness had faded, though, so he tugged out the IV in his hand.

"Mr. Emerson," Nurse Prim said in a startled voice. "You can't do that!"

"I already did," Jax said. He wasn't trying to be a jerk, but he wasn't staying here either. His clothing was folded up on a nearby chair. Kudos to the hospital for getting him undressed and into a hospital gown. "Now if you'll give me a bit of privacy . . . Sonnie."

Her lips flattened, and she set her hands on her hips. "I'll be right back, sir. Please don't try to dress by yourself. If the doctor does allow you to leave early, then I'll send a male nurse to help you with your clothing, and you'll need to be released to a family member who can drive you. Hospital rules."

How hard would it be to convince a Lyft driver to pretend he was a brother? Fifty bucks should do it.

Jax tugged at the tie holding his hospital gown together.

Nurse Prim's eyes widened, and she spun in her white tennis shoes and hurried out of the room. She left the door open a strategic three inches as if he couldn't be trusted behind a closed door. Whatever. Jax had nothing to hide.

Now the room was tilting again. He exhaled, then shuffled to the chair. It took a bit of effort, but soon he was dressed, and his phone and wallet were located. A quick glance at the screen told him he had dozens of missed calls and texts.

Well, he'd seen his dad, his agent, his coaches, and a bunch of his Flyers teammates, and he'd answered a call from his mom, who was on her way back from Europe even though he told her he was fine.

The Pit had about fifty-five texts, and Jax was pretty sure they were all about him and his mishap. The group chat named The Pit consisted of the guys he'd played with on the Northbrook Hockey Elite team years ago, when they were all in high school. Last month, they'd all connected at a fundraiser to help out the club that had given them all their start. Five of Jax's original team had gone pro—well, now six, with the recent signing of Clint McCarthy to the St. Louis Hawks.

Despite some of the differences between the team members, they'd all mellowed over the years, and the fundraiser ended up being a surprisingly good time. Thus, The Pit was born.

He opened the group chat, and without reading a single text, he wrote: *Leaving the hospital now. I'm not in a coma. I'm not out for the season. Since when did you all start believing the media?*

His phone started to ding with replies, but Jax pocketed the thing, because he had a nurse to avoid.

The hospital door opened, and Jax tensed, expecting to see Nurse Prim and the doctor, or perhaps a male nurse or other various hospital personnel there to tell him that he must stay put. Instead, it was a woman who was decidedly not wearing hospital scrubs or any sort of dangling ID tag. No, she wore a cropped white turtleneck above striped trousers that made her legs look a mile long. Her hair was as black as the night outside, and it hung in waves about her shoulders. And she had an elegant, standoffish presence about her. As if she was too good for the mundane things and regular people around her.

He wouldn't be surprised if she was some sort of runway model, the type of woman he stayed far, far away from. Women who had no problem taking bribes from his father. Who had no problem using wealthy pro athletes for their own gains.

But this woman looked like she'd been crying, if her smudged makeup was any indication, along with her red-rimmed eyes. Green eyes with a splash of brown.

Her eyes widened when their gazes connected, and she said, "Oh, I'm sorry, I didn't mean . . ." She stopped talking and simply stared at him.

"I think you have the wrong room, ma'am." He guessed

her to be about thirty, a couple of years older than he was. Was she crying because her family member was seriously sick?

"You're . . . you're *walking*. And you're *dressed*."

Jax furrowed his brow. "I am . . . are you a nurse or something?" Maybe she was off duty? Or just checking in before her shift?

Her cheeks pinked. "Oh, no. I'm . . ." Her green eyes glimmered with tears.

Now what was wrong? She was going to cry again?

"I'm glad to see you up and walking," she continued, her voice trembling now. She was definitely going to cry. "I thought . . . the news said . . ."

Jax folded his arms. This woman was pretty—beautiful, really, in her tragic way—and under normal circumstances he might have wanted to linger and chat despite his aversion to supermodel-type women. But the circumstances weren't usual, and she was a hot mess of tears; besides, Nurse Prim could be back any moment.

"The media sensationalizes things," Jax said. "I'm fine. A bit of bruising, but I'll live."

She took a shallow breath, blinking rapidly. "And your career? It's not over?"

Jax scoffed. "That's to be determined, but not because I was hit by a car today."

The woman covered her mouth, and tears filled her eyes.

Now what had he said?

"I'm so, *so* sorry," she said, sniffling. "I didn't see you until it was too late. I wasn't going very fast, because the light had just turned, and I slammed on the brakes, but it was too late."

It was Jax's turn to stare at her. This woman wasn't in the wrong room. She'd come to see him because she was the one who'd hit him with her car. "*You* were the driver?"

A small cry came from her throat, and she nodded. "I'm so sorry. I didn't mean—"

"Mr. Emerson." Nurse Prim's voice cut in like a shard of glass. She appeared behind the crying woman like a dark cloud. "I spoke with the doctor, and he's cleared you for release as long as you have someone to drive you."

Jax looked from Nurse Prim's stern blue gaze to the watery green eyes of the mystery woman. "My girlfriend's here to drive me home."

"Oh." Nurse Prim turned to the woman. "And what's your name, ma'am?"

The woman's eyes widened. But credit went to her for straightening her shoulders and saying in a steady voice, "Meg Bailey."

Perhaps getting a ride from a stranger who had hit him with her car just hours before wasn't the smartest decision of his life, but desperation called for desperate choices.

"All right, Miss Bailey," Nurse Prim said. "If you can sign here. I also need to see some ID."

Jax watched Meg pull out her driver's license from a silvery-looking handbag slung on her shoulder. Was Meg short for something? Margaret? Megan?

"And your signature, Mr. Emerson." The nurse handed him the clipboard.

He scrawled his name, then said, "Thanks, ma'am."

"Ready, honey?" Jax asked.

Meg blinked those green eyes of hers, an incredulous expression stamped on her face. At least it had stopped her tears.

"Ready," she said, her voice a note above a mouse's.

And with Nurse Prim's gaze on him, Jax moved through the doorway and took ahold of Meg's hand. She didn't resist— and it might be odd to hold the hand of a complete stranger, but her hand was warm and smooth. Not bad for the situation.

They were about ten paces away from the nurse when Jax whispered, "I might need to lean on you a bit. Do you mind?"

Meg looked up at him, worry flashing in her eyes. "Should you even be walking?"

"I'm fine." He released her hand. "The walls are moving a bit, though."

"Maybe you *should* stay the night."

"Hush." He draped an arm about her shoulders, and after a moment's hesitation, she slipped her arm around his waist.

For a willowy woman, she was surprisingly solid and steady, even in those heeled boots of hers. He guessed her to be five-nine without the boots.

He leaned a bit more, and her arm tightened about him. Did he smell vanilla? It had to be her shampoo or her perfume. He wasn't a big fan of cloying perfume, but frankly, anything smelled better than the antiseptic hospital.

They stepped into the elevator, and Jax pressed the Lobby button. He released his hold on Meg and leaned against the elevator wall. As the doors dinged shut, he released a breath. He was on his way. Finally. Yeah, things were still aching and throbbing, but his king-sized bed was sounding like heaven about now. He closed his eyes as the elevator descended. The vertigo was coming back.

"You okay?" Meg asked in a soft voice.

"I'm fine." He'd been saying that a lot tonight. "But a distraction would be nice. Tell me about yourself, Meg Bailey."

She made a sound that resembled a cough.

"Got a cold?" He opened his eyes to look over at her.

"Um, no, I just . . . It's not something I thought you'd ask."

The elevators dinged open.

Meg slipped her arm around his waist again, and they

moved forward as one. Jax spied the hospital exit. Not too much farther. "I don't care what you talk about, but I need to get out of my own head for a while."

"Okay," Meg said as they walked across the lobby, her heeled boots tapping on the floor. "I'm a thoroughbred Chicagoan, born and raised here. After high school, I went through a fashion-merchandising program, then worked in retail for a while. About five years ago, I opened my own boutique."

Jax nodded. "So a businesswoman, huh?"

She shrugged. "Yeah."

"Impressive."

He thought he heard the surprise in her voice when she said, "Long hours are not too glamourous, but I love it all the same."

"That's retail for you, right?"

They reached the hospital exit, and the doors slid open.

"My car's over here," she said.

Jax shouldn't have been surprised to see a small commuter car with a messed-up bumper. Yep. It was the same car that had hit him.

FOUR

GRAY. *SLATE GRAY* to be exact. Meg knew the color of Jax Emerson's eyes. Now that she'd seen them open and up close. She had never been more relieved in her life when she'd pushed open the door of 208 a few inches and saw him dressed and upright. Alive and seemingly all right, for the most part.

And now they were inside her car, and she was going to drive him home. If her life were any stranger, it would be a science fiction novel.

"I apologize in advance that my car's a mess," Meg told the hulk of a man whom she'd supported out of the hospital. With every step, she doubted more and more that she should be helping him out and driving him home. Was there anyone at his place to take care of him? He seemed exhausted, and now that he was settled into the front seat of her car, he'd closed his eyes again.

He hadn't commented on the stacks of shipping boxes in the back seat or the boxes of bracelets she had to move so he could sit down. It wasn't that the car wasn't clean inside; it was just full of stuff she had to transport to the shop in the morning.

"What's your address?" she asked before starting the car.

With his eyes closed, his low voice rumbled out his address.

Meg typed it into her phone, then hit GO on the GPS. Twenty minutes away. Not bad. It looked like he was in a small suburb. She tried not to freak out about the fact that she would be driving pro hockey player Jax Emerson to his home. Or freak out about how he'd held her hand in his huge one, pretended she was his girlfriend, and then used her for support to walk out of the hospital.

Breathe, Meg. "Okay, here we go." She started the car.

Click.

She tried again.

Click. Then silence.

Jax's eyes were open now and focused on her dashboard. "What's wrong?"

Heat crawled up Meg's neck. Last week the battery had died, and she'd had to call roadside assistance for a tow. She should have changed out the battery right away, but then she got the rent increase notice, and everything else got put on the backburner.

"I think it's the battery," she said.

Of all times, of all places, and with all people, *this* had to happen now.

"Maybe it has something to do with the wreck?" Jax asked.

It was an innocent question, and a logical one, but it only made Meg feel terrible. "No, I had to get a jump start last week. I should have replaced the battery right away." She reached for the jockey box, then stopped.

Because two long legs were in her way.

"Um, I need to get the manual out of the jockey box and call roadside assistance," she said. "Your best bet might be to call a Lyft, Mr. Emerson. I don't know how long it will take for assistance to come."

"Jax," he said immediately.

Why did his correction make her feel even worse? As if it was totally normal to be on a first-name basis with the guy she'd hit.

He popped open the jockey box and pulled out the owner's manual. Thankfully, the jockey box was fairly clean. "I could take a look at the engine if you want."

Of course he'd be mechanically minded. Superstar that he was. "No, you look like you're going to fall asleep at any moment, and I'm nearly one hundred percent sure it's the battery," she said. "The car's only three years old, so too soon for major problems, right?"

"Right," Jax said.

She opened the manual, then called the number inside the cover. She should have saved it into her phone. As the phone rang, she felt Jax's gaze on her. Although it was dim inside the car, with only the streetlamps providing light from the outside, she was sure her face was a mess. After crying half the day, she hadn't even dared look in the bathroom mirror.

She gave the hospital address to the woman who answered the roadside-assistance call, then she gave the required info about her car. "Forty-five minutes?" she asked. At nearly one in the morning, that felt like forever. "All right. Thank you."

When she hung up, she looked over at Jax, who was scrolling through texts on his phone.

"Do you want me to book a Lyft?" she said. "I'll pay for it."

Without even looking up, he said, "I'm not going to leave you in the parking lot alone this time of night."

"I'll be fine," she said, because the guilt was carving a giant hole in her stomach. How much more could she take from this man? "The parking lot is bright, and I don't think there will be many muggings taking place twenty feet from the hospital."

"You'd be surprised," he murmured. He clicked off his phone, so the screen went dark. Then he looked at her. Even in the dimness, she felt the intensity of his gray eyes.

"I'm s-serious, Jax," Meg said, knowing she was stumbling over her words. Which all women probably did when Jax Emerson was solely focused on them. "I feel horrible. About everything. And now . . . my car won't start. I'm sure you hate me even more now."

His eyes shifted, scanning her face. "I don't hate you. It took guts to come in and check up on me. Unless you were sneaking in to smother me with a pillow—but I'm betting you're a Flyers fan, being from Chicago and all. I'm just glad you finally stopped crying."

"Definitely a Flyers fan," she said, but her eyes stung. How was this guy being so great to her? So patient? So unfazed? She took a steadying breath. She didn't trust herself to speak, because her throat ached and she felt weirdly shaky. Possibly due to no food or appetite for going on twelve hours.

"Good to know," he said. "Because I'm about to put my life in your hands again. Do you mind if I take a nap until that tow truck gets here? I think the events of the day are starting to catch up."

"Okay," she managed to say.

The edge of his mouth lifted, then he reached around the side of his seat and popped it back. Not that it went very far, with all the boxes in the back seat.

Then, incredibly, he folded his arms and closed his eyes. He was really going to sleep? Now? In her car? He barely fit in it, but somehow he looked comfortable.

"Talk to me," he said, his voice low.

"What?" she choked out. "I thought you wanted to sleep."

28

"I usually fall asleep to the TV, so maybe your voice will work," he said. "Don't be offended if I fall asleep while you're telling me a fascinating story about yourself."

Meg shouldn't laugh. She didn't feel like laughing, but it escaped anyway. "I'm far from fascinating. I mean, I'm the farthest."

His mouth curved ever so slightly, eyes still closed. "Continue."

She exhaled. Alrighty then. So she started to talk. She told him about her brother who was serving in the military and about the grandparents who'd raised them. Her grandpa had passed away a few years before, but her grandmother was as sprightly as ever. "In fact, it was my grandma who always said she believed I could be a shop owner someday. She doesn't get out much anymore, but sometimes I bring her on a field trip to the shop. She loves to browse the clothing and almost always buys a scarf or a blouse."

Jax didn't respond, and she didn't expect him to.

"My grandma's a huge hockey fan, even more so than my grandpa was," Meg continued. "We've spent many a night together with the game on. Well, she watches, and I listen while browsing clothing designers for inventory."

He still didn't respond, but Meg continued, "I don't think I'm going to tell her about this little ... incident. She's probably already seen the news about you."

His breathing had deepened, evened out, and finally she looked over at him. He'd fallen asleep.

"Jax?" she whispered.

No answer.

His arms were still folded, and his eyes remained closed. Remarkable.

She gazed at him. His expression was relaxed, unfettered, unencumbered. With no one else around and Jax unaware, she felt like a spy. Yet he was in *her* car, asleep. She could look at him, right? So she did. From his hands and long fingers—fingers that had clasped hers—to his legs, which were also long and butted up against the dashboard and jockey box, which made her wonder what sort of vehicle he drove. Likely a truck.

Next her gaze moved along his torso. Even a button-down dress shirt couldn't conceal the hard planes of his chest and the leanness of his torso. Or his thick shoulders and sculpted forearms. Jax Emerson was a force to be reckoned with, both on and off the ice. Then there was his face. Had he always worn a beard, since adulthood at least? A lot of hockey players had one, and pro athletes at that. His father had been clean-shaven.

Meg had never dated a guy with a beard, had never kissed a guy with a beard either. Good thing no one was around to see her blush. Where had the thought of kissing Jax come from? If she weren't trying to be quiet, she would have laughed at herself. Jax Emerson was everyone's player in Chicago. His successes were the city's successes.

And those three points he'd scored the night before in the first period had been celebrated by the entire league and the entire city. Had that only been a night ago? Meg rubbed her arms, at the goosebumps there. It was surreal to sit by a man who skated like lightning across ice and could take down 250-pound men with a shoulder bump.

While waiting in the hospital lobby hour after hour, she'd done some googling on him. Read about his roots in Chicago, about his socialite parents, about how he'd been called up pro when he was only nineteen years old. She read a printed interview where he'd talked about learning the game from Coach Fenwick on his club team Northbrook Hockey Elite. It seemed that five of his Sabercats teammates from the club team played pro now. Most recently Clint McCarthy, according to a linked article.

The article had a picture of the group of hockey players at some fundraiser for the club only about a week ago. She pulled up her browser again to look at the saved picture. There was Jax, front and center, wearing a tux that made him look like he could be on a magazine's sexy bachelor list. Yep. She'd googled that too. Jax was single. Some mentions of girlfriends littered the internet, but nothing recent.

Which made Meg even more curious about this beautiful, talented, hard-as-stone man next to her. Why hadn't some gorgeous actress or trust fund starlet scooped him up?

Almost against her will, her gaze moved back to the sleeping Jax. His lips were relaxed, and his lashes rested against his high cheekbones. The slight crook in his nose was probably from a break, or two. His brown hair was tousled, and she realized she'd only ever seen it that way. Helmet pulled off after a game, sweaty, tousled hair.

Well, he wasn't sweaty now. Not that she minded the sweaty version of Jax.

Too bad her car wouldn't start. Even though it was below forty degrees outside, she could use a little AC right now.

Two headlights swung into the parking lot. The bulky outline of the vehicle told her that the tow truck had arrived. She didn't bother Jax; he'd probably wake soon enough. She pulled the hood latch, then stepped out to greet the tow truck driver.

In just a few minutes, her car was started again, and she stood outside, her arms folded against the cold as he ran a diagnostics test.

"Your battery is on its last leg, ma'am," the driver told her. "I'd recommend getting it replaced first thing tomorrow. If it starts up for you tomorrow, that is. I can tow it to the shop if you can find alternate transportation home tonight."

Maybe if Jax weren't asleep in her car, depending on her

to get him home, she would take the tow truck driver up on his offer.

"It's all right," Meg said. "I'll figure it out first thing tomorrow."

"All right then." The driver unhooked his machinery, then swung up into the cab of his truck.

Meg watched him drive away, then with a shiver, she climbed into her car.

Jax hadn't moved.

Good thing he'd already given her his address. Meg pulled up her Maps app and started to drive.

FIVE

"YOU SHOULD SIT this one out, Jackson," his father said into the phone. "Get some rest and your equilibrium back."

Jax clenched his jaw. This was the first time he'd answered a phone call from his dad in a long time. Usually he let calls go to voicemail, then decided if it was worth his time calling back. Since the fiasco with Lacy, things between him and his dad had been strained. And he didn't want his dad to think that just because he'd visited Jax in the hospital, everything was now smoothed over. It was far from that. They still had his contract to talk about.

"I'm already on my way." He'd been home since the accident four days ago. He'd already missed one game, and he wasn't going to miss another. Jax flipped on his blinker and made a right turn. He was ready, and he knew it. He'd been working out in his home gym and been in constant communication with the coach. Since the accident, his teammates had reached out to him more than ever.

Jax felt neutral about this. He'd never been particularly close with his Flyers teammates. He didn't hang out with them socially. In fact, last month at the Northbrook fundraiser, he'd connected more with his old teammates than he had with anyone else over the past eight years in the pro league. Which only told him there were other teams out there, other opportunities.

Life didn't always have to be all about Chicago.

He needed to speak to his dad as soon as he got through this game. About his contract. About how he was going to take control of his career, and life, once and for all.

"Jackson," his dad's voice came again. "One more missed game won't make a difference in your overall career."

"Oh, since you know so much about my career," Jax shot back, "what else do you want to tell me?"

"Son—"

"Look, I need to focus on driving here," Jax cut in. "Your seats are open at the game. Take them or leave them." Then he hung up. It felt good to cut his dad off, to essentially hang up on him. For about thirty seconds. Then he felt guilty for being disrespectful, even though he had every reason to be upset with his dad.

Problem was, there was really no one for him to talk to. No one on his team, not his coaches, and definitely not his mother. He thought about the Northbrook guys. They'd all known his dad had sponsored some of their tournaments, and they'd known he was the rich kid on the team. Yeah, they had razzed him, and Rocco called him Golden Boy, but the guys had never crossed the line, because his dad's money helped them all.

Jax exhaled, feeling stuck. Hockey was his life. Literally. And he loved it. Mostly.

Not the business side of it, that was for sure.

He pulled into his assigned parking space and let the engine idle, keeping the interior of his truck warm while he scrolled through his phone. His dad had sent a text. Of course.

Let's talk after the game. And be careful out there, huh?

Well, if one thing was clear, his dad did care about him. But his personality was so controlling, so stifling, that Jax wished that he had the kind of dad who'd just take him fishing once a month. Simple.

Another round of texts had come in from The Pit. Jax wasn't surprised. Before starting up his truck thirty minutes ago, he'd sent out the text: *Playing tonight. We'll see whose season I can end.*

It was an inside joke—although the wrong type of hit could end another player's season, it was an unspoken code of ethics to never go in for the career-ending injury.

The responses had been fast and furious.

Clint: *I'll watch on my phone because I'm probably going to be warming up the pretty bench in St. Louis.* Clint McCarthy was the newest recruit to the St. Louis Hawks. He'd played in the minor leagues after a four-year stint in the Marines. This season, he'd been called up to the pros. That made two pro athletes in the McCarthy family. Clint's brother Grizz was a professional baseball catcher, originally from the legendary Belltown Six Pack.

Send pics of you on the bench, McCarthy, Zane Winchester wrote. Everyone called him Zamboni, or Z.

Funny, Clint wrote.

Ya, some of us have to actually play tonight, The Rock, aka Rocco De Luca, quipped. He played for the Wyoming Steers. *Show the Chargers what a puck is.*

Hey, Rocco, Dice wrote. Dice, or Declan Rivera, played left defenseman for the Denver Chargers. *When we get done with you, you'll be scraping your teammates off the ice.*

Pull your heads out, Trane Jones wrote. Otherwise known as Diesel, he was the massive goalie for the Michigan Comets. He'd been big at Northbrook Elite, and now he was huge. *We should be congratulating Jax on his miraculous comeback.*

Congrats, dude, Clint wrote. *Recovery from your coma was amazing.*

I didn't get any hospital pics, Rocco complained. *No pics, then it didn't happen.*

Oh it happened, Dice wrote. *You should have heard him whining on the phone the next day. All about how his hip hurt and his shoulder got a few scratches.*

Jax chuckled at this. He scrolled through the rest of the texts, then wrote, *Proof just for you, Rock.* He texted a selfie of himself in his truck, with the stadium visible through the windows.

That started off another firestorm.

Since Jax was a full twenty minutes early, he bantered on the texting group for a few more minutes. Then another text came in. One not part of The Pit.

Meghan. She'd signed her first text *Meghan,* so he knew her full name now.

When she'd dropped him off at his house the other night, she'd walked him to the door. Then after a debate of whether or not she should pay for his hospital bills, in which he'd said no and she kept insisting, he finally told her to give him her number and he'd call her if he needed anything.

"Anything at all," she'd gushed. "I can take out your trash, bring you dinner, anything."

He'd raised a hand to stop her crazy offers. "You're not taking out my trash."

But he'd called her the next day. She hadn't answered, so he'd left a message that he was perfectly fine and didn't need any help with trash. She must have called when he'd taken a nap, because he'd woken up to a voicemail from her. Basically apologizing and reoffering to help him with anything at all. He'd called her back. Voicemail. She'd called him. Voicemail.

What had followed was a series of texts, mostly Meg

asking how he was doing and offering to help and Jax saying he was fine but thanks for checking in.

This text, though, was different.

Heard you're playing tonight. Good luck, Jax. I'll be watching with my grandma and crossing my fingers for you.

It was sweet. And now he was wondering if she'd told her grandma about the accident. Probably not. And that was fine. He'd told both his agent and his dad to drop the subject. Except for the healing road rash and the occasional twinge in his hip, there was nothing to think twice about.

He had started to reply to Meg's text with a standard thank you when he paused. Maybe if he called her now, she'd pick up. The text had come in only a few minutes ago, so he pressed SEND on her number.

On the third ring, he was about to hang up when she answered in a breathless voice, "Hello?"

"Meg?"

"Yeah."

"Were you, uh, running or something?"

"No," she said. "I was just . . . well, I was on top of my grandma's counter, dusting her cupboards. When my phone rang, I might have tried to get off the counter too fast, and I might have slipped, and then . . . well, you know the rest. I didn't want you to have to leave another rambling message. This phone tag thing has gotten old."

Now Jax was smiling. "My messages are rambling?"

She hesitated, and her voice was lower when she spoke. "A little."

He swore he heard the smile in her voice. "Well, I think yours are too short. You don't tell me sorry nearly as many times as you should, and you've only offered to take out my trash about fifteen times."

"That bad, huh?"

Jax was grinning. Sitting in his car by himself, grinning. "But I do appreciate the offers, though I think you can stop now."

"Oh." Did she sound disappointed? "'Cause you're all better?"

"I'm all better," he said.

"Yeah, that's what the media said." She gave a small sigh. "I mean, not that they're reliable, but I thought I'd wish you good luck anyway. In case you need it. Do you need it, Jax Emerson?"

She'd used his full name in the messages she'd left, and he decided that he liked it.

"I'm never opposed to someone wishing me luck," he said.

A sports car whizzed into the parking lot. Lucas was here, and Jax watched the huge goalie get out of his tiny car. Lucas didn't even look his way, which was fine with Jax. He wasn't looking for a grand entrance.

"It's almost ready, Grandma," Meg said in a muffled tone. Then, more clear to Jax: "The pre-game talk is starting up, and she wants to eat in front of the TV."

"You cooking?"

"I am," she said, her voice coy. "And I'd bring you dinner if you let me. But it seems you're too *fine* to accept anything from me."

"Like I said in my texts, I'm not opposed to dinner, but not as an apology."

"Yeah." Her tone was softer. "I read that, but I wasn't sure what you meant."

Jax really shouldn't do this. In fact, he should tell her thanks for watching the game and to have a nice life. Without him. Instead, he said, "I was thinking of dropping by your shop and checking it out. Then maybe after we could get something to eat. Or you could cook for me. I wouldn't be opposed to that."

The silence on the other end of the phone lasted way too long to be normal. Maybe her grandma was talking to her again? "Meg?"

"Pro hockey players don't just drop by my boutique," she said. "I mean, we don't sell menswear."

He really wished he could see her face. "I think you're missing my point, Meghan."

"Okay, then, come by the shop," she said quickly. "But I'm paying for dinner, and you aren't going to change my mind. When do you think you'll come?"

"No can do," Jax said.

"You're not coming now?"

"I think it would be better if I surprise you."

She laughed. A nervous-sounding laugh. "Oh, it will be a surprise. Just prepare yourself for my employees fangirling over you."

"Employees?"

"Yeah, Nashelle works full-time, although I don't even think she knows that hockey is a real sport. But my part-timers will probably faint on the spot if they see you come into my shop."

Jax chuckled. "That would be a first. But what about you, Meghan? What will you do when I come see you?"

"I think it would be better if I surprise you with my reaction," she quipped.

Bumps raced along his arms. She was flirting with him, definitely flirting. "Touché."

The thump of a loud bass to a rap song preceded the sighting of Corbie, the other starting forward on the team. His black SUV practically vibrated with the thumping beat he had cranked up.

"What's that?" Meg asked.

"You can hear it?"

"Yeah."

"Corbie is here," Jax said. "Time to get inside and change."

"Oh, right," Meg said. "Well, good luck again."

Jax had to go, but he didn't want to hang up. A buzzer sounded on Meg's end of the call, and then another muffled something to her grandma.

"Hey," Jax said. "If you ever want to come to a game, I'll get you tickets. Bring your grandma."

"Oh . . . okay," Meg said. "She doesn't like to go out much at night, but maybe if it's in the afternoon, I can drag her there."

The teasing in her voice made him smile. "Don't make me bribe you."

She laughed. "If anything, I could bring one of my fangirl employees." She paused. "Thank you, Jax. That's sweet of you."

When Jax hung up with Meg, he wondered when he'd last been told he was sweet. He didn't mind it coming from Meghan Bailey.

SIX

"HERE YOU GO, Gran." Meg set a tray of food on the coffee table. She'd made lasagna, garlic bread, and salad.

"Thank you, dear." Grandma wore her faded Chicago Flyers jersey and had on her glasses—which meant she was ready for the game. She'd also done her hair and makeup as if they were going out. It made Meg smile.

"I didn't want to miss the announcement about Jax Emerson," her grandma said. "He's going to be playing tonight, you know."

"I know." Meg arranged a plate for her grandma, then handed it over to where she sat in her easy chair, making sure there were plenty of napkins to catch any spills.

"This smells heavenly." Grandma cut into the lasagna on her plate. She took a bite, then said, "It's wonderful, dear, but who were you talking to in there?"

This question made Meg pause. She could blow it off, say it was one of her employees with a question . . . But what if Jax really did give her hockey tickets? That wasn't something she'd hide from her grandma.

"I have something to tell you, something you might find hard to believe."

Her grandma finished chewing a bite of lasagna. "Not much surprises me anymore."

This will, Meg thought. She took a deep breath. "All right, you know how I said I'd be staying over at the shop the other night?" Sometimes when she had inventory, she'd sleep in the back room because she didn't want to drive home for just a few hours, then have to return early.

"Yes, you had extra work because Nashelle had been sick."

"Well, that part was true," Meg said.

"Are you saying you fibbed, Meghan Bailey?" Grandma used a napkin wipe her mouth.

Despite being thirty-two years old, Meg could still be chastised by her own grandmother.

"I'm sorry, Gran," Meg said. "It was complicated and—"

"Did you use birth control at least?"

Meg's mouth fell open.

"You know that protection is essential, even if it's one time. Young people these days do things out of order. They don't marry before making love. Don't think I'm naïve, young lady." Grandma cut another piece of her lasagna and proceeded to take another bite, as if she hadn't just stunned Meg.

"I wasn't with a man," Meg said. "Well, I was, but it's not what you think. That dent on my bumper wasn't from a parking lot. I hit a man when he was crossing the road."

Grandma's eyes rounded like a startled cat.

Meg continued, telling how she'd called the ambulance, then gone to the hospital and waited all day for Jax Emerson to be alone, how she drove him home while he slept in the car, how they'd been texting and playing phone tag over the past several days, and how fifteen minutes ago, he'd offered her tickets to one of his games. The only thing Meg left out was

Jax saying he was going to stop by her boutique, because she doubted that would really happen.

The announcer's droning voice on the TV was the only sound after Meg finished with her long, convoluted tale.

Grandma's gaze had fallen to her plate of lasagna. When she lifted her hazel eyes, she said, "I could go to a night game, dear. I'd just have to take a nap first since I'd need more energy than sitting at home. I don't have one foot in the grave yet."

Meg's thoughts buzzed. This was Grandma's answer to everything she'd told her? That she wanted to use Jax's tickets?

Meg bit her lip to hold back her smile, but it escaped anyway.

"Turn it up, dear; they're talking about your Jax now."

Your Jax. Meg turned up the volume. The announcers were talking about the miraculous comeback of Jax Emerson, and from that moment on, Meg was glued to the screen. Behind the announcers, the players were warming up on the ice, and she immediately picked out number eleven.

"Jax Emerson declined to speak to us before the game, but we have his agent here, Scott Jenson, who will answer a few questions for us."

Meg realized that Scott was the second man she'd seen in the hospital, after Jax's father. He definitely looked like a man who enjoyed facials and manicures. He basically repeated what the announcers had already said, then he added, "I think you'll see a softer side of Jax after this experience. Sometimes we don't appreciate what we have until we're close to losing it."

"Isn't that the truth," the announcer said. "It happens to all of us. Hockey's only a game, after all."

Meg stared at the screen. Something felt off. Like they were dictating how Jax should act. As if there had been something wrong with him before. She glanced over at Grandma, but she didn't seem fazed.

43

By the time Meg cleared dinner and did a quick round of dishes, the national anthem was being sung. Meg joined her grandma as the starting lineup was announced. When Jax Emerson's name was called, her heart rate went wild, mimicking the cheers of the fans in the arena. He raised his hockey stick in acknowledgment, and the crowd went wild again.

"They sure like him," Grandma said with a chuckle. "Are you sure you know what you're getting yourself into?"

Meg glanced at Grandma. "What do you mean?"

Grandma pointed a finger at the TV. "That boy is no bookworm like Blaine. Going out with him will not be a quiet life."

"Jax hasn't asked me out," Meg said. Or had he? Besides, Blaine was old news. Months old. "And maybe I don't want a repeat of Blaine. After all, we're not together anymore."

Her grandma had liked Blaine. They'd spent hours doing puzzles together and talking books. Their split had hurt her grandma too.

But Blaine always had his own agenda. What they did on weekends, where they'd eat, who they should hang out with . . . it had taken awhile for Meg to notice. But once she'd realized that everything was about Blaine and what he wanted to do and what he liked, the rose-colored glasses had faded.

He'd even talked her into buying a larger apartment, just in her name, and he'd promised to move in and pay half. That had never happened. She'd bought the apartment, but he'd never moved in. Things had ended between them soon after the closing date.

"I don't like to see you hurt," Grandma said. "But being on your own isn't good either."

Meg exhaled a patient breath as she tried to ignore the reminders that her grandma had given her about her pathetic dating life. No, she hadn't been out with anyone since Blaine.

She'd been extremely busy. Mostly. It probably had something to do with the fact that she and Blaine had been together for about three years, and he was always content with where their relationship was. No marriage proposal on the horizon, although Meg had hoped.

Until the day all her hope had come crashing down.

Blaine had told her he was seeing someone else.

Two weeks later, she'd heard from a friend that Blaine and his new woman were getting married soon. Meg had proceeded to unfriend their mutual friends on social media. He was likely married by now, living his happy life without her, but she didn't have to see the pictures to prove that her heart had been broken into a dozen pieces.

Six months was plenty of time to get over someone, right? To start dating again, to start opening her mind to new possibilities.

Seconds after the hockey game started, Jax had the puck under his command. It was a beautiful thing to watch him so effortlessly glide over the ice, maneuvering around the opposing team, passing, then receiving the puck again to make the shot.

Goal!

The arena went crazy, and Meg jumped to her feet and squealed. "I can't believe it!" She wrapped her arms about her torso, hugging herself. Jax had scored in the first minute of the game. Amazing.

"That's your boy," Grandma said.

Meg didn't correct her, because she was too busy staring at the man on TV. Jax was back, and he'd just proved it in front of thousands of fans. She hadn't ruined his career. He was fine. Absolutely fine.

Still smiling, Meg settled onto the couch. The Flyers scored in the second period, then in the third. Neither was by

Jax, but Meg didn't care. She was just happy that he was on the ice, making plays.

It was surreal to think that she *knew* Jax Emerson, had talked to him on the phone before the game. He had said he'd stop by her boutique. And wanted to take her out for dinner. The game ended, and the media was a firestorm, mostly talking about Jax's comeback. Meg had never smiled so much in her life. Then the announcer said, "Sheila is on the ice with Jax Emerson right now. We'll cut to Sheila and hear from the man himself."

The camera switched to an angle near the team's bench, and sure enough, a dolled-up journalist held a microphone between her and Jax. He'd pulled off his helmet, and his hair was a sweaty mess.

"First of all, congratulations, Jax," the reporter said.

"Thanks, Sheila," Jax said.

"Tell us how you're doing after your accident," Sheila continued, her lipsticked smile wide. "We were all cheering for your comeback, but it's like you were never injured."

Jax scrubbed a hand through his hair and leaned closer to the microphone, his slate-gray eyes boring into the camera. "Honestly, Sheila, being hit by a car was better than being hit by Rocco."

Sheila laughed. "That's Rocco De Luca, folks, plays for the Wyoming Steers. Is he the one who broke your collarbone last season?"

"The very same," Jax said with a crooked smile.

"You're playing the Steers next week," Sheila continued. "Will there be some payback from last year?"

"Nah." Jax high-fived another player who moved past him. "Rocco and I go way back. We've had our run-ins on the ice, but we've always been friends off the ice."

"Most of your club team went pro, right?"

"The answer is yes as of last month, when Clint McCarthy signed with St. Louis," Jax said. "And that reminds me. This weekend, we're holding the first Sabercats Youth Hockey Camp at the Northbrook Elite Hockey Club arena. My former teammates will be joining me, and we're limited to only one hundred spots. Sign-ups are through the Northbrook website."

"Sounds like an amazing opportunity for kids interested in hockey who want to learn from the pros," Sheila said in her peppy voice.

Jax's gray eyes zeroed in on the camera. "The event is open to the public, so anyone can come and watch."

Meg swore he was looking directly at her. She drew a throw pillow against her stomach and squeezed it against her, as if she could stop the butterflies that were circling inside her.

"There will be a small entrance fee," Jax continued, "but all proceeds go toward the club hockey scholarship fund. The event was organized by Bree Stone, who recently started up Prime Outreach Incorporated, an amazing nonprofit organization that helps fund athletics for kids and communities."

Surprise showed in Sheila's eyes, likely because she hadn't been prepared for the conversation to change directions. "Did you hear that, folks? A great opportunity for Chicago kids. Just visit the website to find out more."

"The Northbrook Hockey Elite website," Jax clarified.

"Right." Sheila grinned into the camera. "Back to you, Robert."

The post-game coverage continued, but Meg wasn't listening much anymore. Her skin buzzed with happiness for Jax. He'd been at the top of his game, and she couldn't be more pleased. She wished she could talk to him or text him or something. But that would be pretty bold.

Yet . . . what would it hurt to text him a congratulations?

47

The butterflies were bouncing again as she considered it. Maybe she should do it now, when she knew he wouldn't see it for a while. Wouldn't they be showering, then maybe doing some sort of after-party?

"Well, I think I'm going to turn in, dear," Grandma said. "I have a busy day tomorrow, and I can't stay up like I used to."

Meg hid a smile, because her grandma always said she had a busy day the next day. And she supposed Grandma did stay active, with quilting and puzzles and books. "All right, Gran, sleep tight."

Grandma chuckled softly. "I know *you* will be having nice dreams."

Meg stared after her grandma shuffling out of the room. Meg should be grateful that Jax was at least a distraction from Grandma talking about Blaine so much.

Meg pulled her knees up on the couch and drew a fuzzy blanket from the back of the couch over her legs. She indulged in scrolling through the texts she and Jax had exchanged over the past week. They were super brief and to the point. But after her last text, he'd called her. More butterflies danced.

She typed out a text, then deleted it, then retyped something shorter. Might as well stick with the status quo. *Congrats on the goal and the win. Good luck at the hockey camp.* SEND.

She didn't expect him to reply right away, and he didn't. In fact, she wondered if he would reply tonight at all. She wouldn't stay up and wait, but she wasn't really tired. So she browsed some online clothing-designer shops to see when they were showcasing their upcoming spring lines. The major designers had already debuted their lines at the New York fashion week in September, but Meg wasn't after the big designers. She liked to discover up-and-coming designers or small designers with a unique flare.

A sigh escaped as she realized she should be looking not to increase inventory but to consolidate and find cheap rental space for warehousing purposes. Her thoughts strayed to Jax, and she ended up searching for more articles on him. She clicked on the Wikipedia link and froze. He was only twenty-eight, which meant she was four years older. Hmm.

He seemed older, but she should have known. There was always a wrinkle with her and the guys she dated. Before Blaine, she'd dated a guy named Carson. He'd lived with his parents still. Before that, Richard—who liked to play both sides of the field. And her first boyfriend out of high school—Lance—had been arrested for embezzling money from his real estate job.

So her track record was pretty lame, and that was why, at thirty-two, she was still single.

Her phone rang, startling her out of her haze of thoughts.

Jax.

He was calling. At midnight.

Breathe, Meg, then answer in a normal voice.

"Hello?"

"Hey."

That was all it took to wake up the butterflies in her stomach. "Great game."

"You should come to the next one." His voice was low, raspy, like he'd been yelling or talking all night. Or simply kicking butt in a hockey game.

Meg burrowed deeper into her fuzzy blanket. "I think I will. My grandma says she's up for it too."

Jax chuckled, and Meg let the sound ripple across her skin.

"Consider it done," he said. "We're playing the Wyoming Steers, so you can meet Rocco."

Meg sat up on the couch. Rocco De Luca was the player

Jax had talked about in his interview after the game. He wanted *her* to meet his former teammate? "Okay." Had her voice squeaked? "When's the game?"

"Monday night."

Four days suddenly felt like forever. "Sounds good." Yeah, her voice was definitely squeaky. "My grandma will be ecstatic."

"What about you, Meghan?"

She laughed. And blushed. The way he called her by her full name made her toes curl. "Are you fishing for compliments, Jax Emerson?"

His laugh was warm and deep.

Meg pushed off the fuzzy blanket. Way too hot now.

"See you soon," he said in that low voice of his.

"Okay." How many times could she say okay in one conversation? And then the call was over. Meg, of course, had already started to analyze every word he'd spoken. *What about you, Meghan? See you soon.* What did *soon* mean? Monday? Or would he really come by her shop?

SEVEN

JAX HAD LOOKED up Meg's Loft on his phone before heading over to her shop, or boutique, or whatever she called it. So he knew it would be closing in about thirty minutes. He could hang around and maybe talk her into dinner. It had been less than eighteen hours since he'd talked to her after last night's game, and he'd thought of her for about twelve of those hours. Unless he counted when he was sleeping too, because when he woke up, she'd been on his mind.

The Northbrook guys were all flying in tonight since the youth hockey camp was tomorrow. So The Pit was already chiming with plans to meet up for a late dinner. Jax wasn't committing to anything since he wasn't sure how things would go with Meg ... not that he was planning on an extended evening with her, but he was keeping his options open. Besides, he'd see all the guys bright and early tomorrow morning.

Now Jax pulled his truck into a parking lot from across the shop. The sign for *Meg's Loft* glowed blue against the dark winter night. Closing time was 7:00 p.m. on Saturday, so that should give them time to hang out and eat before Jax redirected to the Northbrook guys. Right?

He gazed at the storefront for a moment. The large window displayed three mannequins wearing satiny or sequined dresses that looked much too cold for Chicago in December. Maybe they were party dresses for Christmas or New Year's?

He shut off his truck when a couple of texts chimed in.

What about Romero's Homestyle Restaurant? Dice wrote. *Yelp says it's amazing.*

Uh, leave the restaurant choices to us Chicagoans, right, Jax? Clint replied.

Agreed. None of those tourist traps.

As long as there's BBQ, Zane wrote. *I'm craving it. What's up with the snow here? I didn't know I had to pack an Eskimo coat.* Zane must have landed already, coming in from Tennessee.

This is nothing, Clint wrote. *Chicago's having a mild winter so far.*

Stop complaining, Tennessee boy, Rocco said. *Download a weather app or something.*

Jax chuckled, then put his phone on silent. These guys could go on forever, and as entertaining as they were, Meg was only across the street.

He climbed out of his truck and pulled up his hoodie because it was rather cold and the wind had picked up. Then he crossed the street, after looking both ways for cars, of course.

The shop was warm, and the scent reminded him of Meg—vanilla and cinnamon and something sweeter—but she wasn't in sight.

"Can I help you?" a woman asked, looking up at him. Way, way up, because she couldn't be more than five feet tall.

The woman appeared to be in her mid-twenties with about eight layers of eyeliner. She wore all black, and her equally black hair was twisted in some sort of funky bun with two decorative sticks poking out.

52

"Looking for a gift? Your wife, perhaps? Or sister?" The woman pointed to a rack of long flowy things. Were they dresses or skirts or shirts? "These just came in from Nerve, a designer from Canada. We only have one size in each color, so tonight is the perfect time to buy. I'm assuming she's tall, but if she's not, that's all right too. We do carry petite sizes in most everything. Insisted on by me, of course, since I always wear petite." She was barely breathing. "Or our popular lounge pants are thirty percent silk, and we have them in the most gorgeous winter colors. Yeah, I know what you're thinking. Pale pink and seashell blue are winter colors? That's fashion-forward thinking for you."

Jax rubbed at his beard, wondering when it would be a good time to cut in and ask after Meg. It seemed he'd just encountered her top saleswoman, perhaps in all of Chicago.

"What's her hair color?" the woman continued. "Most women don't know their season, but if you can tell me her hair color and her complexion hue, then I can tell you her season and help you pick out the perfect—"

"Nashelle," another woman said. "Can you help me with—"

The voice stopped, and Jax turned.

Meg's eyes widened. "It's you . . ."

"Who?" the woman named Nashelle said.

Jax tugged back the hood of his sweatshirt. "It's me."

"Who?" Nashelle said again.

Would it be rude to ask her to just go away?

"Uh." Meg's green eyes seemed darker than a forest. "Nashelle, this is Jax Emerson, a . . . friend of mine."

Nashelle set her small hands on her miniature hips. "Jax Emerson? Sounds familiar." She looked at Meg. "Why is that name familiar?"

"He plays hockey for the Chicago Flyers."

Nashelle bit on her lip, which happened to be covered in black lipstick.

Thankfully, Meg wasn't wearing black lipstick, because Jax decided he didn't like it. No, Meg's lips were perfectly . . . rosy. And her hair was braided and hanging in a long tress over one shoulder. She wore a deep-red long-sleeved shirt and some sort of patchwork vest over it. Her short skirt revealed her long legs, covered by red-print tights.

"No, that's not it," Nashelle said. "Are you a singer by chance? Maybe I've seen you at Brando's Speakeasy on Dearborn?"

Jax wanted to laugh. "No, I don't sing in public."

Nashelle shrugged. "Well, whatever. You got this, Megs? I've got that date tonight with that guy I met on Tinder."

"Sure," Meg said. "Thanks for your help today. See you Monday."

Nashelle blessedly, mercifully, walked to the back of the store somewhere, out of sight.

When Jax moved his gaze back to Meg, he hoped she didn't think he was laughing at her employee, but what had possessed her to hire such a person?

"Sorry about that," Meg said in a rush. "I should have given her a heads-up, but I didn't know if you were coming, or when, or . . ." Her voice trailed off as Jax stepped closer to her.

It was really good to see her again. And he caught her vanilla scent, like her store. "Interesting tights."

The blush that bloomed on her cheeks might have been too gratifying, and Jax couldn't help smiling.

"Um, thanks. I guess." Her gaze did a slow perusal of him. "You know, if anyone but Nashelle had greeted you, they might have thought you were a gangster."

His brows lifted, and he moved a step closer. "Is *gangster* even a word anymore?"

Meg's eyes filled with laughter, but she didn't laugh. She rested her hand on a nearby rack. "It is in this part of the city."

"Sorry I didn't dress for shopping in a fancy store."

Meg did laugh then. "We don't have a dress code, but you're . . ." She waved at his person.

Jax looked down at his jeans and tennis shoes, then he met her gaze again. "I'm what?"

"Sort of a big, intimidating guy." She folded her arms.

"Nashelle sure didn't have a problem selling the new lounge pants to me."

Meg smirked. "Well, you still look expensive, even if you are just wearing a hoodie and jeans."

"Expensive?"

Her blush was back, and he noticed that her eyes weren't solely green but had some brown in them too. So, hazel then.

"You know." She waved a hand again. "You definitely don't shop at a discount store."

Jax looked about the boutique. He guessed that nothing inside the place was cheap. "And you would know, being in the clothing industry."

"Correct."

"So what do you recommend?" he asked, closing the distance between them and examining the rack she was leaning against.

Faint lines appeared between her brows. "For what?"

"My mother. Although I don't think she'll like those flowy things. She's more into the tailored stuff."

This clearly surprised Meg. "You're here to shop?"

He couldn't resist teasing her. "Of course." Jax leaned close and picked off a small string that was on her braided hair, then he lingered, his gaze on her. "Why else would I be inside a women's clothing boutique at seven o'clock on a Saturday night?"

Then he moved away and began to look through clothing as if he'd truly come to buy something.

The bell over the door tinkled, and a woman bustled in.

"Can I help you, ma'am?" Meg said immediately.

Jax glanced over to see a fifty-something woman who looked like she owned stock in the diamond business, if the glittering jewelry at her ears, neck, wrists, and fingers were any indication.

"I need a hostess gift," the woman said in a stiff tone. "I'm running late to a benefit and nearly forgot. Do you offer gift wrap?"

"We do," Meg said. "Are you looking for a clothing item, such as one of our handwoven silk scarves, or perhaps a pendant fashioned after the Renaissance era?"

Jax was standing right next to a table display of scarves, and he assumed they were the ones Meg had referred to. "My mother loves scarves too," he cut in. "Do you think I should get her a color for every season? I think she's autumn."

Both women spun around and looked at him.

Maybe he'd gone too far?

Meg's brows arched in surprise, and the customer's ice-blue eyes narrowed as if he'd spoken out of turn, which he had.

Then the customer's mouth fell open. Her eyes widened, and that's when he knew. The woman was a—

"Jax Emerson! Oh my goodness! I didn't know you shopped here!" Diamond Lady literally rushed to him, and he had to take a step back because he was suddenly afraid of what she might do. "That goal last night was amazing. I told my Pete that you're on your way to getting league player of the year."

And, yep, her long, manicured nail poked him in the chest.

"Would it be too much trouble to take a selfie with me? Pete is just going to die."

Jax cleared his throat. "That would be fine, ma'am."

He caught Meg's stunned expression at the edge of his vision. He sent her a *help me* look, but she didn't budge, didn't intervene. She didn't even offer to take the picture. Meg merely observed as Diamond Lady pulled out her equally decorated cell phone from her giant shiny purse, then looped her arm through his.

"Smile," Diamond Lady said.

Just as she snapped the picture, her other hand squeezed his arm. "Goodness, you *are* strong."

He thought he heard Meg giggle. Why wasn't she helping him? He didn't mind fans in general, but there was really nowhere for him to escape to right now. So he might as well get the woman buying something and on her way.

Diamond Lady turned so that they were very, very close to each other. "You're the same age as my son, but he's not athletic at all. No, he's a computer programmer." She sighed. "I guess we can't all get lucky."

Jax had no idea what she was talking about, but he needed to put some distance between himself and this woman. "Maybe you can suggest a scarf for my mother." He stepped away from her and walked to the other side of the table.

"Oh, that would be wonderful." And just like that she began to pick through the scarves on the table. She held up one after the other, discarding some and creating a small collection with others.

Well, maybe this would take longer than he thought. Hadn't she been in a hurry?

"That one's perfect," he said about the next one she held up. "And it's her favorite color." He didn't even know what color he held in his hand. Some sort of orange red.

"I think I'll get the same one too," Diamond Lady said. Something beeped on her phone, and she looked at it. "Oh, goodness, I'm going to be late." She clasped her hands to her chest. "It was so wonderful to meet you, young man. You tell your mother I hope she enjoys her gift."

Diamond Lady followed Meg to the register, and within a few minutes, she'd waltzed out of the store, waving goodbye to Jax.

When the door shut behind her, Meg said, "Wow. Does that happen a lot?"

Jax rubbed the back of his neck. "I've had some interesting run-ins, but that might have topped them all."

Meg locked the door and turned the open sign to closed.

"You're locking me in?"

"We can take the rear exit." Her mouth lifted at the edges.

"You're assuming a lot."

She smirked, but she walked toward him. "Are you really going to buy that scarf?"

Challenge accepted. "I am. How much?"

"One hundred seventy."

He tried not to look surprised, but he failed.

"I can give you the owner's discount if you want."

"No, I'm just not familiar with women's clothing prices, and this seems like a piece of fabric."

Meg reached him and took the scarf from his hands, her fingers brushing his. "It is a piece of fabric, but it's also hand-woven silk."

"Right." He watched her walk to the cashier desk. The print on her tights was little swirls, like half circles that didn't connect. He forced his gaze higher before she turned around. He decided that she fit into her surroundings. Meg was elegant and stylish yet mysterious somehow, much like the clothing on the racks and hanging from the walls.

"Will that be all, Mr. Emerson?" Meg asked, tapping something into the register.

Jax took his time walking to the counter. Then he rested his palms on the flat surface. "I believe we had dinner plans?"

Meg's gaze lifted, and in her eyes he saw something he liked a lot—interest.

"I thought you were here to shop," she said in a coy voice.

"Are you busy?" he asked.

"I'm always busy."

He pulled out his wallet. "Are you hungry then?"

She smiled. "I'm paying."

Jax nodded and slid his credit card across the counter. He'd take what he could get. "Deal."

EIGHT

WAS SHE REALLY doing this? Climbing into Jax Emerson's truck while he held the door for her? She was pretty sure she'd had a mini heart attack when she discovered the man Nashelle was speaking to was a six-five pro hockey player. There to see *her*. No matter what he'd said about shopping.

And now he was walking around the front of his truck, carrying one of the Meg's Loft bags with his purchase.

It was zany. It was surreal. This didn't happen in real life. Not to her.

She'd texted her grandma that she was going out with a friend for dinner, and her grandma had texted back: *Enjoy time with your boy.*

The driver's side door popped open, and Jax climbed in, then started up the truck. He adjusted the heater vents and turned up the heat. Strangely, Meg wasn't all that cold, although it had to be around thirty degrees.

A warm shiver traveled the length of her body that had nothing to do with the cold and everything to do with the man next to her. His scent had filled the truck, all masculine and spice mixed with pine.

"Where are we going?"

His gaze flashed to hers before he pulled onto the street. "Are you a salad girl or a pasta girl?"

"Either-or, maybe both?"

Jax nodded. "There's a little place not far from here. It's quiet, but good."

"No crazy fans?"

The edges of his mouth lifted. "I can't guarantee that, but there's a back booth that's pretty private."

Meg's pulse jumped at the thought of anything private with Jax. She decided not to overthink it, because if she did, then she probably would stop breathing on the spot.

Jax had been right—the Italian restaurant was tiny, but the moment they stepped inside, Meg knew it would be delicious. The aroma of fresh bread and marinara sauce wrapped around her. The place was about half full, and no one paid them much attention as a waiter led them to their table.

Their booth was by the kitchen, but it was separated from the rest of the place, which gave them privacy from the other restaurant patrons. "Do you want me to take your coat?" Jax asked.

She wore a lightweight down coat, but it would get too warm quickly. "Sure." She drew it off her shoulders, and Jax slid it the rest of the way, the tips of his fingers brushing against her arms. He set her coat on the end of the circular bench.

Jax motioned for her to go first, and she slid about halfway around the circular booth. He tugged off his hoodie, and his T-shirt rode up, flashing a bit of his torso.

Oh wow.

Where was the ice water? She picked up the menu and scanned the choices without reading a word as Jax slid into the booth next to her. Well, not right next to her. About two feet away. Still. Sitting this close to him was doing crazy things to her pulse. She could smell his spice-and-pine scent, hear his breathing, and practically feel the warmth from his body.

His muscled forearms were propped on the table, and Meg couldn't help peeking at the definition, born of years of hockey.

"Good evening." Their waiter was back. "What can I get you to drink, folks?"

Meg ordered water, and Jax ordered water too.

When the waiter left, Meg looked over at Jax. "Water? I'm surprised."

"Need to stay hydrated," he said. "Plus maybe I like surprising you."

She tried to focus on his gray eyes, but her gaze kept straying to his shoulders, to the length of his arms, to his fingers . . . His fitted blue T-shirt seemed to be made for his exact dimensions. "As long as they're good surprises." She picked up her menu—she needed the distraction from all that was Jax. The menus looked like they'd seen better days, but at least there were English words along with the Italian.

He opened his own menu, and she glanced at his wrist. He wore a different watch than he'd had on the day of the accident.

"What do you usually order?" she asked, dragging her gaze back to the menu.

"Lasagna is sort of my go-to."

No way.

"What's wrong?" he asked, his lips curving upward.

She blinked. She'd been staring at him. Again. "That's sort of my specialty. In fact, I made it last night for dinner, you know, for my grandma. I make several different kinds."

"You're kidding me."

She shook her head.

"Then what are we doing here?" he asked. "Do you have leftovers?"

Meg held back a surprised laugh. "I think you'd give my grandma a heart attack. She'd need a lot more notice."

"Tomorrow night then?"

This time she did laugh. She didn't know if he was teasing, but she couldn't imagine a world in which Jax Emerson walked into her grandma's house, ever. "Um, don't you have that youth hockey camp thing?"

"Yeah." Jax was still looking at her, completely ignoring his menu. "But it's over at five."

Okay, so those gray eyes of his were boring straight into her soul, and she wondered if anyone had ever told this man no. "My grandma's probably having leftovers right now, so if I made lasagna tomorrow, that would be three days in a row."

Jax's gaze moved over her face, and she was pretty sure she was going to blush.

"I don't see a problem with that, do you?"

Meg reached for her ice water and took a small sip, feeling Jax's gaze on her every movement. "I think you're a man who's used to getting his way, Jax Emerson."

"Is that a yes?" he asked in a low voice.

"It's a *maybe later.*"

He threaded his fingers through his beard as if he was in deep thought. "I can live with that."

Would it look obvious if she used the menu to fan herself?

"Are you folks ready to order, or do you need another minute?" the waiter asked, reappearing suddenly as if he was waiting for the slightest break in the conversation.

"We're ready," Meg said quickly. "I'll have the, uh . . ." She scanned the menu. Maybe there were more things in Italian than she'd realized.

The waiter waited. Jax waited.

"You order first," Meg said, glancing up at Jax to see an amused gleam in his eyes.

"I'll have the classic lasagna with extra parmesan bread," his voice rumbled.

Then it was her turn again. There was no way she could make a decision with the two men waiting for her, so she took the easy way out. "I'll have that too, but with salad instead of the bread."

When the waiter left, taking the menus with him, Meg drank more of her water.

"You're really thirsty, huh?" Jax said.

She set down her water and folded her arms. Again, Jax tracked her every movement. Was it a hockey player thing, or was he an intensely observant man?

"I am thirsty," she said, defending herself. "And the water's really good."

He nodded, his eyes amused. "Have you always lived with your grandma?"

"You mean, why would a thirty-two-year-old woman live with her grandma? After my grandpa died and my grandma had to have a double knee replacement, I was going to move out of my apartment and stay with her for a bit. But my boyfriend talked me into putting money down on a two-bedroom. Said he'd pay the lease until my grandma was better, then we'd, uh, live together there. Things went south between us, though, and I didn't want to move into a place with memories of him, or us, so I decided to rent it out."

His brows lifted. "You're thirty-two?"

"Is that all you got out of my spiel?" Might as well get it out in the open. "And you're what . . . twenty-something?"

"Twenty-eight."

Yeah . . . she knew that.

"I'm an old woman compared to you," Meg said, not sure if she was kidding or not.

Jax draped his arm across the bench behind him and turned more toward her. "You're not old."

"Four years is a big difference," she said. "I was driving when you were in sixth grade."

He smiled. "When you put it like that."

She playfully shoved his chest. But he was rock solid and didn't move an inch.

"Maybe I like older women," he said, still smiling.

She really liked his smile. Were they really doing this? Flirting? Meg reached for her water again, Jax's eyes not leaving her face. "Do you, um, usually bring older women here?"

"You're the first," he said.

His fingers strayed to her braid, and although he didn't touch her skin, she could feel the warmth of his fingers anyway.

"Maybe that's my problem," he continued.

"With what?" she asked, because him touching her braid was really distracting, and she was having trouble following his conversation.

"With my past relationships," he said. "You know, dating women younger than me. They're immature and don't see much past my career and income. Maybe I've been looking in the wrong places and I should have been looking to the older, more established type."

Meg leaned her head back, which put more space between them. Jax's hand dropped, but his fingers were about an inch away from her shoulder.

"The older women *do* seem to like you. That lady in my shop would have probably asked you out if she hadn't been married."

He chuckled. "I don't mean *that* old, no offense to Diamond Lady, or whoever she was."

Meg smiled. A heartbeat of silence passed between them, and she knew she had to ask him the big question. "Why are we here, Jax? I mean, you should hate me, or at least not want to have anything to do with me. But you've been . . . understanding. Sweet. And you've gone way above and beyond any expectation by any standard."

"A beautiful woman's buying me dinner. What more could a man want?"

She scoffed, although the compliment had sent a horde of butterflies spinning in her stomach. "You've turned down all my apology offers, and then suddenly you show up at my boutique."

He hooked his finger around her braid. "I don't know exactly," he said in a low tone. "And that's the truth. But I do know that I find you interesting, intriguing, and I want to figure out why. Yeah, we met in an unconventional way, but I don't hold any grudge against you."

Meg released a breath. "So I'm sort of like a research project?"

His fingers brushed against her shoulder. "Sort of."

Now she had goosebumps racing down her arms. "Are you ever going to tell me where you were going in such a hurry that day?"

For the first time all night, his gaze shifted away from her. "I had some bad news," he said in a low voice, "and it was already a crappy day. I wasn't focused on where I was going. I didn't even see your car."

When he didn't elaborate, she said, "So I made your day worse?"

His gaze cut to hers again. "Maybe you saved my day. If

67

I hadn't been knocked out and taken to the hospital, I might have done something rash and jeopardized my career."

This was not what she expected him to say. "That serious?"

It was his turn to drink some water, but he didn't move away from her.

"My dad ... well, I found out some things about my contract, and it shocked me, when in fact, maybe it shouldn't have shocked me at all."

Meg didn't intend to take his hand, but somehow her body acted on its own, and she grasped his hand near her shoulder. "I'm sorry," she said. "For whatever it was."

He nodded, then he linked their fingers together.

Meg tried to ignore the heat racing through her. She'd only meant to comfort him, simply offer a listening ear, but nothing with Jax Emerson was simple.

"Your lasagna, ma'am." The waiter had returned.

Meg drew her hand from Jax's and turned reluctantly toward the food on the table.

"Smells great," Jax told the waiter.

Since Meg could see that the lasagna was piping hot, she started on her salad, but Jax didn't wait on his.

They ate for a few moments in silence. It wasn't an awkward silence, though. Meg wanted to ask him a dozen questions, about what the bad news had been, why his father was so involved in his career, and why it had already been a crappy day for him.

"Is it as good as yours?" Jax asked.

Meg looked up from her plate. She'd only had one bite of the lasagna. "It's a close second."

"Oh, you're killing me," Jax said. "How about I pay tonight, and then you'll owe me something like a homecooked meal. We'll give your grandma plenty of notice."

Meg wiped her mouth with a napkin. When she'd offered to bring him food after the accident, it had been to his place while he was convalescing . . . having him over for dinner at her grandma's house was a whole other matter.

"I'm sure my grandma would be thrilled," Meg said.

Jax's mouth twitched. "And what about her grand-daughter?"

"She would be fine with it."

Jax shook his head, but he was smiling.

"But I'm still paying tonight."

NINE

JAX HAD NEVER told anyone he'd dated about his complicated relationship with his dad. Not the history or the details. So when he found himself opening up to Meg as they sat in his idling truck outside of her closed shop, he surprised himself. Maybe it was because she had told him about her deadbeat parents, and how her mom had hooked up with some other man and her dad had gone off the deep end after that, leaving her grandparents to raise Meg and her brother.

Jax could tell it was something she didn't talk about much, especially when she told him that all of her girlfriends were married, with kids, so really the only social interaction she had now was when one of her friends went through a divorce. But that ended quickly enough when the next man came along.

So Jax had told her about his ex-girlfriend, Lacy, the one he'd thought would be different. It turned out she was worse than everyone else.

"Well, I'm glad you found out who she really was before you married her," Meg said.

"Yeah, I should be glad too," he said. "It took me a long

time to even speak to my dad after that. We've only been on cordial terms. Nothing more. The first time we had an in-person conversation for months was at the hospital."

"Well, maybe your dad's learned his lesson," she said, and before he could refute that, she added, "At least you weren't with Lacy for three years like I was with Blaine. He never proposed, though, so maybe that was the red flag I ignored."

"Three years, huh?"

"You didn't think I was just hanging around being single for so long, did you?"

"I'm surprised you're single now."

Meg smirked. "I know, what's not to love?"

"I haven't found anything to scare me off yet," he teased.

"Okay, you're way off topic here, Jax Emerson," she said. "Tell me about your growing-up years."

Nice detour. "My parents were the very definition of helicopter parents—mostly my dad, though. He had no relationship with *his* dad, so I think he became overzealous when I was born, trying to prove himself or something."

He felt her gaze on him in the darkness. And if they were talking about pretty much anything else he might have leaned over and kissed her. Yeah. He wanted to kiss her. Not that he'd tell her that. She seemed hung up on their age difference, since she'd brought it up a few times during dinner. But Jax found he didn't mind at all.

"And you're the only child," Meg said. "So your dad's attention can't be divided, right?"

Strangely, Jax was comfortable with her questions. Maybe because she truly listened. It was something he liked about her. She heard everything he said and didn't miss a beat.

"That's true," Jax said. "If he and my mom had a better relationship, maybe he'd be with her more. As it is, they basically live separate lives. My mom has her friends, her music, her art, and she's often traveling. Whereas my dad's firmly situated in Chicago, coming to all my games and running his businesses."

"Does your mom come to your games?"

"When she's in town." It was fine, it really was. He couldn't expect his parents to be coming to every game, not when he'd been playing the sport since he was a kid. A good twenty years now.

He looked over at Meg. She'd pulled her feet up under her. She looked relaxed and comfortable, and he liked that. He liked her. She was beautiful, yes, but she also had an aura of calm and peace about her. Which he had found out tonight in her boutique. Maybe it was maturity and being older than him, but she was also quiet, in a good way. Not a loud, brassy, or pushy woman, but someone who thought through things before acting with confidence.

"How did you get started in hockey of all sports?" Meg met his gaze. "I mean you could have probably played anything."

"My dad played, and it was his way of dealing with his own demons," Jax said. "But he never competed beyond high school. He told me he was on the cusp of playing in the minor leagues, but he was cut. Went to college instead, majored in finance, and now he uses his money to get what he wants."

"And to control others."

"Exactly." Jax exhaled.

"Can you talk to him about it? Man to man—"

Jax gave a short laugh. "Believe me, I've tried."

Meg merely nodded, not pushing him. "Maybe it's his love language. You know, buying you things, helping you out financially."

"You don't understand," Jax said. "My agent told me that my dad donated money to the Chicago Flyers."

"As a sponsor?"

"I'm not exactly sure, but I want to get my lawyer to look into it," Jax said. "My agent says my dad donates the exact amount of my contract each year. Three million dollars."

Meg's intake of breath told Jax that she understood what that meant. She shifted closer. "You're an amazing player, Jax. Your career had been stellar, and if you didn't play for the Flyers, you'd be playing somewhere else, right? Still making those points and—"

"I don't know, Meg." He rubbed the back of his neck. "I don't know if I would have been offered by another team. The Flyers was the first one, the *only* one at the time, and I thought I was the big man in Chicago to get an offer right in my hometown. But now I find out that my dad might have bought my way onto the team. Who knows, maybe he added a little extra to bribe the coach to make me a starter."

Meg grabbed his hand from his neck and tugged it toward her. Then she clasped his hand between both of hers. "I think you need to talk to the coach and find out if the donation was made legally, before you bring in your lawyer."

Jax looked at his hand in hers, then met her gaze. He liked that she'd taken the initiative. He liked that she wasn't afraid to offer up her opinion. "You're probably right. Because if the donations aren't legal, then my dad could be prosecuted."

Meg moved closer and leaned her head against his shoulder, still keeping his hand in hers. She didn't say anything, and he didn't move, because his pulse was doing crazy things. It was too soon, he knew—too soon to kiss her. To do more than hold her hand. Her scent of vanilla and cinnamon was like an aromatherapy, and it was quickly becoming his favorite scent in the world.

"I hope it's not that serious," she said in a soft tone. "For your family's sake."

Jax nodded.

When she yawned, he said, "I didn't mean to keep you out so late listening to my woes."

Meg lifted her head and squeezed his hand. "Sorry, I'm not usually such a baby."

Their gazes connected, and everything inside Jax told him to kiss her, but he held back. He didn't want to presume she was attracted to him as he was to her.

"No problem," he said. "I'll probably stop in and say hi to the Northbrook guys—they're at a hotel together, and they're not taking no for an answer."

"I haven't even heard your phone."

Jax pulled it from his pocket. The screen showed two missed calls and thirty-two texts.

"Oh wow."

"It's the group chat," he said.

Jax popped open his door and held it open for Meg to scoot out.

She was sitting in the middle anyway, so it was closer to the driver's side door.

When she landed on the pavement, she looked up at him. "Good luck tomorrow," she said, taking a step away from him, toward her car.

"You should come." The look in her eyes mirrored his own surprise. He wasn't used to being so spontaneous.

"To the hockey camp?" Lines appeared between her brows. "What would I do?"

Jax shrugged. "Hang out. You know, see my old digs. I could introduce you around."

She didn't answer for a moment, merely gazed at him as if she was trying to determine his motivation. Hell, he didn't even know his motivation. But it would be cool if she came.

"I'm doing inventory tomorrow," she said, but her tone was easy.

"Well, if you finish early, stop by."

Her mouth curved into a smile, then she stepped forward and wrapped her arms around his neck.

He pulled her close. Yeah, his heart was racing, but it wasn't that kind of hug. It was more of a friendship hug, which was fine with him at this point.

"Thanks for everything, Jax," she said against his ear, her breath warm. "And whatever you do, don't quit hockey."

She released him and stepped away then. He had no response whatsoever. How did she know that exact thought had worked its way into his psyche? How did she know he'd lost sleep over it for several nights in a row? She couldn't know, that's what.

He watched her walk the short distance to her car—the one with the dented bumper—and climb in, then drive away. He wasn't sure how long he stood beside his truck, but when snowflakes began to fall from the sky, he finally climbed back in.

Twenty minutes later, he walked into a swanky hotel bar with thumping music. A few couples were on the dance floor, but most of the patrons were at the bar, save for one set of tables where five guys were all seated.

The first one to notice him was Dice. "Jax! It's about time!"

Dice rose to his feet and greeted Jax with a bro hug and solid slap on the back.

"Don't dress up for us," Clint said, shaking his head.

Yeah, so Jax was the only one in a T-shirt and hoodie. "Didn't want to upstage you, Fido." Everyone laughed at Clint's nickname. It had carried over from his Marine days, and since his St. Louis team had started using it, so had the Northbrook guys.

The Rock pulled Jax into a tight hug, then kissed him on

the cheek. It was part of his Italian culture, and the guys were used to it by now. "Looking forward to tomorrow night," Rocco said. "Get ready to wipe your teammates off the floor."

"We'll see who needs the broom," Jax teased.

Rocco slapped him on the back, and Jax moved to Zane, the most mature of the lot at the table. As a single dad, he had a more serious perspective of life. "How's little Hope?" Jax asked after clapping Zane on the back. Hope was his five-year-old daughter.

"She wanted to come," Zane said with a laugh. "I told her in a couple of years, and that she'd have more fun with my aunt and uncle."

"She's welcome anytime," Jax said.

"Thanks, man," Zane said, sincerity in his tone.

"Bring it in," Declan said, rising to his feet.

"How are you, Dice?" Jax asked. "How's your mom?"

"She's putting up a fuss," Dice said with a grin. "Doesn't want to move to be near me. But I think I'm wearing her down."

"Keep working on it," Jax said. Dice's mom was recently widowed. "She'll be glad she did when all is said and done."

Dice slipped his hands into his pockets. "Thanks, dude. I hope so."

"Good to see you, Emerson," Diesel said next. The biggest guy of the lot, Trane Jones was one of the top goalies in pro hockey. He was formidable on the ice, but his heart was as good as gold.

"You too, Diesel."

"All right," Zane said over everyone's conversation. "Now that Jax is here, it's time for the announcement."

A hush fell over the table.

Rocco let out a low whistle.

"It's nothing like that," Zane said, although his face was strangely flushed. "Clint, your turn."

"Thanks, Z," Clint said. "I have some good news. I called Coach when I got into Chicago, and he agreed to come tomorrow."

Jax blinked. He'd reached out to their former club coach, Hal Fenwick, last week, but he hadn't been able to make it. Huh.

"Nice," Jax said with a slow clap. Everyone else joined in. It would be good to see the man who had set a different example of what it was to be a man, one who was pretty much the opposite of Jax's dad.

"Annnnd . . ." Clint drew out the word. "My brother Grizz tweeted the event on Thursday and Friday."

"Woot! Woot!" Rocco called out.

Dice whistled, and the other guys hooted and clapped.

Grizz McCarthy was Clint's older brother. He played pro baseball and was a phenomenal catcher. The guy had over a million followers on Twitter. With the added publicity from Grizz, the Northbrook arena could very well sell out tomorrow.

"Hey guys, I hate to do this to you, but we need to get a picture together," Jax said. "Then we should all post it to our Insta or Twitter or whatever."

A couple of good-natured groans circled the table, but a moment later, Jax had stretched out his arm and taken a selfie with the other five crowding behind him. Then he texted the picture to the group chat. He uploaded it to his Instagram and added a line about the camp, then tagged the Northbrook Hockey Elite Club page.

He pocketed his phone, and for the next hour he talked and laughed with his former teammates. After his talk with Meg and all his confessions, he felt lighter somehow, as if he didn't always have to be alone in his issues with his dad. He knew that not all of these guys had stellar home lives growing up. Some came from broken families, and Diesel had a pretty dismal upbringing with an abusive father. He'd been a scholarship kid to the club and was practically a son to Coach.

It was nearly one in the morning by the time the group broke up. They'd see each other bright and early in the morning. Jax didn't check his phone again until he was in his truck, warming it up. Nothing from Meg. Not that he expected her to text him or anything. It wasn't like they were really a thing. Still, he felt oddly disappointed.

Then he switched over to Instagram and saw that he already had about two hundred likes and several dozen comments on his post of the team picture. One of the most recent comments was by an Instagram account named Meg's Loft.

Jax clicked on it.

Good luck tomorrow, it read, followed by a blue heart emoji.

Jax wasn't sure how long he had stared at the blue heart, but when he finally pulled out of the hotel parking lot, his truck was plenty warm.

TEN

THE FIRST THING Meg noticed about the Northbrook Hockey Elite Club arena was that the place was freezing. She'd left her coat in the car, but now she didn't know what she'd been thinking. There was only about an hour left of the camp, at least according to the website schedule. She'd gotten a good part of inventory out of the way and decided what she could resell wholesale, what should stay in the store for the time being, and what she'd discount for the website.

Her online orders were usually slow, but she just needed to add features to the site to make it more competitive, such as free shipping and emailed return labels. She should also sell some basics like camisoles and hosiery. It seemed her love of fashion was going more commercial.

She wondered if she'd find a seat. She walked through the portal and paused to scan first the arena, then what was happening on the ice. The moment she caught sight of Jax backwards skating with a group of about ten kids, her heart started thumping. He wasn't wearing a helmet, and even from her position, she could see his strong profile. He wore a dark-green jersey that said *Northbrook Elite Sabercats* and skating pants, but no pads. She watched him move with such grace and agility and a confidence born of someone who'd spent years on the ice.

She found a seat smack in the middle of about row fifteen, then settled in to watch. It was obvious who the other pro hockey players were—huge guys who were doing an incredible job of being patient with the kids of all ages. As she watched Jax talking to his group of kids, the memories of the night before flooded back. Him in her boutique, his teasing at the Italian restaurant, then his personal confessions while they sat in his truck. That hug. His arms around her had made her feel so protected. If he'd kissed her, she knew she would have welcomed it. But he hadn't, and maybe her hug had been too forward. Yet it had felt right. There was no denying it. And that made her nervous enough.

Maybe I like older women, he'd said. *I find you interesting, intriguing, and I want to figure out why,* he'd said. *You should come tomorrow,* he'd said.

Now that she was here in an arena full of people, she wondered if he'd just been friendly. There were a good couple thousand people here. What did it matter if she was here or not? Or had Jax been sincere when he'd told her he found her interesting and intriguing? *Was* Jax Emerson interested in her? It was surreal to think about.

Then Jax looked up into the stands, and for a second, she thought he'd spotted her. But that was crazy. How could he pick her out among all of these people? Of course, this was Jax Emerson, who seemed to have eyes in the back of his head and could guide a tiny puck across the ice with barely a flick of his hockey stick.

Anyway, his attention was now back on the kids. Maybe she'd imagined that he'd noticed her. Meg dug her hands deep in the pockets of her jeans. At least she was wearing a wool sweater, although the merino was more for softness and style than it was for true warmth.

A whistle blew, and an older guy who couldn't possibly be a current hockey player motioned for everyone to join him in the center. He held some sort of microphone he spoke through, telling the kids about the next phase of the camp. The coach's voice boomed, and everyone in the arena could hear it.

Meg scanned for Jax again. He'd moved to the side of the arena that she was sitting on. He was talking to a guy that was huge—if possible, bigger than Jax himself. The huge guy was definitely one of the pro players.

She pulled up the website with the camp info on it, and matched the pictures to the guy talking to Jax. Trane Jones, goalie for the Michigan Comets.

When she next looked up, Jax was looking at *her*. This time there was no doubt. He lifted his hand in a half wave. Heat shot through her, and she waved back.

"Do you know Jax Emerson?" someone next to her asked.

Jax was now skating toward the group of kids, and Meg looked over at the woman.

"Yeah, I do," Meg said lamely.

The woman, probably in her mid-twenties and all decked out with fake lashes, plumped-up lips, and a lowcut sweater that left little to the imagination, gave Meg a onceover. "Oh, wow. You his older sister or something?"

"Uh, no," Meg said, getting annoyed now. "He doesn't have a sister."

The woman's painted brows rose. "Don't tell me you're dating him, because he's not dating anyone. My cousin knows his teammate Bones, and believe me, Jax Emerson's way out of your league, honey."

Meg could only stare. Who talked this way? Especially to a stranger. Meg had no response. None at all. But she couldn't sit here listening to this bizarre lady who thought Jax was up for discussion.

She rose and moved through the row, going the opposite way of the crazy lady. When Meg got to the aisle, she headed toward the portal that would lead to the concourse. Her cheeks felt hot with embarrassment. No, she wasn't dating Jax, and even if they were, how was that anyone's business?

She should just leave, but when she got to the concourse, she leaned against the wall. Maybe she'd overreacted. Still, she could probably go. Jax had seen her, waved, so what more would happen?

She and her grandma would go to the game tomorrow night. From there, she had no idea.

Her phone buzzed with a text, and she glanced down at it, surprised to see it was from Jax. *Where did you go?*

Meg texted back: *It was pretty crowded. I'm going to take off.*

Don't leave yet, we're almost done.

Okay, wow. Meg glanced at the time on her phone. There was at least thirty minutes left. He wanted her to wait for him? She blew out a slow breath. No, she wasn't going to read into this, at least not more than she should.

Okay, she wrote.

Great, meet me in Portal A.

Meg didn't move for a moment. He really wanted her to wait for him. This was not what she had thought might happen. She'd planned to check out the camp, then maybe the next time they talked, she'd bring it up.

But this . . . was much more official.

She looked for the portal and found it at the end of the arena. It was completely empty, but by the time the camp ended, she realized it was where the coaches and players came through from the locker room. She leaned against the wall and focused on her phone. *He's not dating anyone,* the woman in the stands had told her. Jax had talked about his last girlfriend, Lacy, and how that had ended in a disaster.

Had he not dated since then? He'd said it had been about a year since the breakup. Meg pulled up her Google search bar and typed in *Jax Emerson Lacy*. No articles came up, but in Google Images there were some pictures. Lacy was blond and beautiful in a Barbie-like way. Pretty much the opposite of Meg. She clicked on the first picture, and it led to Lacy's social media. All the pictures with Jax in them were over a year old.

Meg kept searching, this time on Jax's social media profiles. Twitter, Instagram, Facebook. He was only active on Instagram, where he posted pictures of random hockey stuff, including the one from last night that she'd commented on. Any pictures he was tagged in that had other women in them were clearly platonic. Huh. So maybe he hadn't been dating. Maybe his heart had truly been broken by Lacy. Or maybe he just didn't have time or hadn't found someone *interesting and intriguing*?

A warm shiver danced across her skin as she thought again of the way Jax had been last night. So attentive. Touching her in small ways. Playing with her braid. Linking their fingers when she'd grasped his hand. Pulling her close when she'd hugged him.

Footsteps in the portal brought her attention up. One of the hockey players was coming toward her, a duffle bag slung over his shoulder. He was fully focused on his phone as he walked past.

Another player entered the portal. But this one slowed his step as he neared. He was a tall, sandy-haired guy, good-looking in that Scandinavian way. "Well, hello there," he said with a crooked grin. "Waiting for someone?"

Was he a teammate? He looked familiar, then she realized he was one of the Flyers. His name was on the tip of her tongue.

"Don't worry, I'm used to it," he continued.

"Used to what?"

"Oh, you aren't speechless in my presence," he said with a wink.

Was this guy for real? "I was just trying to remember your name—Nate Rochester, right?"

His smile widened. "Right. But you can call me Razor, everyone else does." Another wink. "Who is a pretty woman like you waiting for?" he asked, stepping closer.

Since Meg was already leaning against the wall, there wasn't really anywhere for her to go.

Nate was at least as tall as Jax but maybe not as broad. Still, he was in her space.

"I'm waiting for Jax," she said.

"Is that so?" Nate said, his blue gaze scanning her face, then dipping lower. "I didn't know Jax was keeping a little hottie under wraps."

Meg's neck prickled with heat. She folded her arms. "I think this conversation is over."

Nate's eyes flashed with mirth. "Ah. A tiger, I like it. No wonder Jax has been keeping you out of sight." He lowered his voice. "If you don't like talking, texting is just fine with me."

She said nothing, but she didn't drop her gaze.

Nate gave a slow nod, his gaze again combing over her. She wanted to slap him just for looking at her like that.

"How about it?" he prompted.

"How about what?"

He shrugged innocently. "You know, give me your number, and when you're done with Jax, hit me up. Or during. I'm not picky."

"I don't think so."

Nate laughed. "I'll make it easy, sweetheart. Just give me your phone, and I'll do all the work."

Then, to her shock, he pulled the phone out of her hand.

For a stunned moment, she didn't react, then before he could type anything into her contacts, she grabbed the phone.

But Nate was faster, and his huge hand clamped around her wrist. "Now, I was just trying to be friendly, sweetheart. But I can play dirty too, if that's how you like it."

"What the hell are you doing?" someone said.

Nate went spinning away from her. And suddenly Jax was there, his back to Meg. Somehow with one motion, Jax had Nate pinned up against the wall.

She lost her hold on her phone, and it went tumbling to the ground. But that was the least of her concerns. Nate's face was turning bright red with the pressure that Jax had at the guy's throat.

"Easy, Jax," another guy said, this one shorter, but broader than either man. He had to be Rocco.

Meg had no doubt Rocco could take everyone out.

"Don't touch her, *ever*," Jax ground out, oblivious to everyone but Nate.

Nate tried to swallow, but it was more of a choke. "Sorry, man. Didn't know she was your girlfriend."

"It doesn't matter who she is. You don't ever grab a woman like that."

Nate's eyes bulged. "It won't happen again," he rasped. "I swear."

"Jax," Rocco said, landing a heavy hand on Jax's shoulder. "You're cutting off his air."

"I don't give a shi—"

"What's going on?" someone else said.

An older man had arrived on the scene, the coach Meg had seen on the ice.

It didn't take long for the coach to assess the situation. "Lay off, Jax, I'll handle this."

Only then did Jax loosen his grip.

87

Nate gulped for air, his face still red, but more from anger and embarrassment now. "Payback's gonna suck," he ground out as he scooped up his duffle and strode away.

"I'm looking forward to it," Jax called out after him.

"Dude," Rocco said. "Wanna play for the Steers tomorrow night? I think that guy's got your number."

Jax's stormy gaze flicked to Meg, then over to the coach. "Sorry you had to witness that, Coach. But Nate was manhandling Meg."

Coach looked at Meg, his brows raised. "You okay?"

Meg wasn't sure she could talk, but somehow she managed. "I'm fine." She bent and picked up her phone. It seemed to be in one piece, but she could examine it later.

"You know there's zero tolerance for violence off the ice," Coach said, but his words held no reprimand.

"I'll gladly pay the consequences," Jax said, his gray eyes stormy.

Coach looked at Meg again, then back to Jax. "I think we can put this one behind us." He clapped a hand on Jax's shoulder. "I've got to sign out some of the kids. We'll talk later."

Jax gave a brief nod.

Coach strode off, and Jax looked over at Meg. "What did Nate say to you?"

Meg swallowed. "He was just being cocky. Then he asked for my number, but I wouldn't give it to him."

His jaw flexed. "Rocco, can you give us a minute?"

"Sure thing, man," Rocco said. He nodded to Meg. "Nice to meet you."

She opened her mouth, but no words came. Rocco strode away without giving her a chance anyway.

Then it was just her and Jax in the portal.

"Sorry about that," Jax said. His voice was more even, and his eyes weren't so wild looking.

She wasn't sure if he was apologizing for his or Nate's behavior, but the adrenaline running through her had left her shaky.

"Tell me what he said," Jax said, his tone almost normal now.

Meg slipped her phone in her bag, then ran her fingers through her hair. "He, uh, he asked who I was waiting for."

Jax's eyes narrowed. She might as well tell him everything. There was obviously no love lost between the two teammates.

Jax remained absolutely silent as Meg rehashed the conversation. "Then you came, and well, I think he got the message." She hoped to see Jax soften, but there was no sign of it.

"Look, I'm fine," she continued. "I promise. Nate's just a jerk, and I'm a bit out of my element here—with all these pro athletes around. Maybe I need to learn the lingo or something."

"There's no lingo, and there's no excuse for what he did."

Meg nodded, drawing in a shaky breath.

"Come on, let's get out of here."

This brought Meg up short. "Where are we going?"

"Wherever you want," he said, scanning her as if he was double-checking she hadn't been harmed. His phone rang, and he looked at it. "Hang on."

While he answered, Meg's mind spun. Jax was taking her out . . .? Had he been planning this since he saw her in the stands?

"I'll catch up with you, later," Jax was saying. "You can tell the guys that something came up. I'll see them on the ice when our teams play each other."

After he hung up, Meg said, "You had plans with your friends?"

"They have plans," he said. "Mine have changed."

Meg sighed. "I'm not going to come between you and your Northbrook team. How often do you guys get together?"

Jax shrugged. "I saw them last month at a fundraiser. We've been together all day, though."

She couldn't read the expression in his gray eyes, but she knew she'd feel guilty if he ditched his friends. They'd be leaving soon, and she . . . well, she was here. "Go with them. I've got some website stuff to do anyway that I've put off too long."

His brows drew together. "We could go eat, then you can do your website stuff."

"Really, I'm fine, Jax," she said, placing a hand on his arm.

He looked down at where she was touching him, then he met her gaze.

"I'll see you tomorrow, at the game," she said. "With my grandma."

One side of his mouth lifted. The spark in his gaze sent a warm shiver through hers. "Are you sure?"

"I'm sure."

"Okay, but I'm walking you to your car."

They headed out the exit nearest to the portal, which meant they weren't intercepted, because a crowd of people had collected where several of the players were gathered by the concessions. It looked like the players were signing autographs.

The wind had turned icy, and Meg folded her arms against the chill.

"No coat?" Jax asked.

"I left it in the car," she said. "I didn't think the arena would be so cold."

Jax shrugged out of his fleece-lined denim jacket.

"You don't have to do that," she said, even as he set his jacket across her shivering shoulders. "My car's just over there."

"You're going to get sick if you don't stay warm."

She eyed him in the Sabercats jersey. "What about you?"

"I run hot," he said. "Besides, I have a strong immune system."

This made Meg laugh, despite her shivering. "Oh, really?"

"Really." He was smiling, and this was a good thing.

She was happy to have the Nate Rochester incident behind them.

Meg dug out her key fob from her purse and clicked to unlock the doors of her car. "So that was your club coach?"

"Oh, yeah, Hal Fenwick. Sorry I didn't introduce you to each other."

They'd reached her car, and she turned to him. He stopped near the car, near her, his hands in his pockets.

"Maybe another time," she said as nonchalantly as possible. "Rocco seems nice."

Jax's mouth quirked. "I don't think I've ever heard that adjective when it comes to Rocco. But maybe he's only nice around the ladies."

"I can tell he's a good guy."

Jax's nod was slow, and he placed a hand on the hood of her car, bringing them closer together. "He's a bit of a hothead, but I can overlook that most of the time."

Meg arched her brow.

"What?" Jax scanned her face.

Was he leaning toward her?

"I think that's a kettle calling a pot black," she said.

Jax's mouth lifted into a half smile.

She had the sudden urge to touch the beard on his face,

just to see what it felt like. But she should probably get in her car right now. And give him back his jacket, because it reminded her of him. Warm and solid.

"I think it's the other way around," Jax said in a slow voice, his gaze moving to her mouth. "It's a pot calling a kettle black."

"Whatever."

He chuckled, and she was pretty sure in that moment he was going to kiss her. In public. In a freezing cold parking lot.

But someone honked a few rows down. Tires screeched, followed by another honk. Nothing like being plunged back to reality.

"Thanks for the jacket," Meg said, slipping it off and handing it over. "And good luck in your game tomorrow. My grandma and I will be cheering."

Jax took the jacket, but he didn't move.

Okay then. Meg turned and opened the car door.

He held it as she climbed in.

"See you soon, Meghan Bailey," he said before she pulled it shut.

She gave him a half wave through the window, then started her car. Without looking back she drove away. She didn't want to think about what might have happened if no one had honked. And she didn't want to think about the way Jax Emerson made her feel—like she was the only woman he saw—or how she found *him* intriguing and interesting. She wasn't naïve. Jax could have his choice of women, amazing women, women who weren't about to lose their business and women who knew how to blend into the world of pro sports.

ELEVEN

JAX ROTATED HIS neck as the national anthem keyed up. Then he stood stock-still, his gaze on the American flag. Nate had been watching him all during warmups, and Jax had completely ignored him. He had no problem taking things to the next level; he just wanted to know when and where.

Jax would never forget the sickening feeling in his gut when he saw Nate grab Meg's wrist, and the look of panic on her face. If Rocco hadn't been there, Jax had no doubt he would have made Nate pass out at the very least.

Clenching his jaw, Jax tried to focus on the soaring music and the triumphant words. No such luck. Tonight was a birthday party for Lucas, their goalie, but Jax would happily ditch it if Nate was planning on going too.

And Jax had set up a meeting with the head coach tomorrow morning. It was time he got to the bottom of his contract.

The only good thing about tonight was that they were playing Rocco's team, the Wyoming Steers. Oh, and Meg and her grandma were in the stands. He'd have to meet her grandma after the game. Jax had thrown in a few more tickets, and Meg had invited the rest of her staff, and he could only guess the women sitting next to her dressed as if they belonged on a New York runway were the employees. Nashelle was also there, in her signature black with gobs of dark makeup making her look like a reincarnated vampire. Of course, he'd keep that observation to himself. The petite woman scared him a little.

It should be a relatively good night, all things considered. Although the Steers were two steps ahead of the Flyers in the national standings, Jax planned to change that tonight.

The lights in the arena dimmed, and spotlights sprouted all over the arena as music boomed through the complex. The announcer began to make player introductions against the backdrop of screaming fans, and the team skated onto the ice to wild cheers.

After the thunderous announcing was over, Jax skated to his position, keeping Rocco in his line of vision. And since Rocco was right wing and Jax was left wing, they faced each other dead-on as the game whistle blew. Roof, the Flyers center forward, passed to Jax, and he dipped it backward to Nate. They might have had words yesterday, but they were still on the same team, although Jax would be ready for any cheap shot coming his way.

It didn't come yet, and Nate zigzagged to the side, edging past Rocco.

The Flyers fans went wild, and the Steers goalie hugged the net.

"I'm open, Nate," Jax yelled.

But Nate took the shot, and it glanced off the goalie's pads.

Jax would let this one go, but nothing more.

Rocco took advantage of the Flyers' distracting stomps, meant to mimic a herd of Wyoming steers, and zoomed past Nate and Jax, heading straight for the Flyers goal.

Lucas was ready, though, knowing his work would be cut out for him tonight. He deflected the shot, and by the time

Rocco circled around, Jax was in his way.

Bones went to work, taking command of the puck, and Jax skated past three Steers toward the goal. One clipped his shoulder but not enough to alter Jax's course.

Bones passed to Corbie, and Jax yelled, "Open!"

Corbie passed at an angle, so Jax only had to connect and change the direction a few degrees. The puck slipped beneath the Steers' goalie's knees just before he hit the ice.

The arena erupted, and Jax grinned as he skated past Rocco. "That's your first lesson," Jax called out.

Rocco's expression didn't change. The Rock was immovable on the ice, except when Jax was on a mission.

Corbie slapped Jax's helmet. "Nice job, man! Let's do it again."

The game continued at a furious pace, neither team letting up. By the time the first period buzzer sounded, the Flyers were up by one. Nate had missed three shots on goal, and Bones had taken a pounding from a Steers player.

The locker room break was a cacophony of congratulations and pep talk by Coach Lindon, but Jax stayed quiet, focused.

His fresh jersey on, Jax headed back to the ice. He took a second to scan for Meg. Sure enough, she was there, in conversation with her grandma. The older woman looked like she was in hog heaven, wearing a Flyers jersey and holding a giant tray of nachos. Jax let a smile escape, but then it dropped when he saw his dad sitting three rows down. Why wasn't he in his box seats?

As usual, he had his cell phone to one ear while plugging his other ear with his finger. Probably some business call.

"Excuse me," someone said, then shoved past Jax so hard that he careened into the plexiglass.

Nate didn't look back.

Jax bit back a curse and grabbed his hockey stick from the bench. The sooner Nate learned his manners the better, but they had a game to play right now.

The second-period buzzer rang, and it seemed that the Steers had sucked down energy drinks during the break. Rocco was on fire. He scored four minutes in, and the arena groaned.

"Shake it off, Lucas," Jax called. "Stay focused."

"Do something," Lucas retorted.

Nothing to take personally, Jax knew, but that didn't mean Lucas wasn't frustrated. They all were. The game was tied up. Nate took ahold of the puck next, only to get slammed by Rocco.

Nate spun and crosschecked Rocco.

Big mistake. Rocco went down. The ref blew the whistle, but no one on either team heard it. Jax pulled Nate from Rocco, which Nate didn't appreciate. The guy turned on Jax, fists flying.

Jax shoved Nate backwards. He went skidding, but not before using his stick to undercut Jax's legs. Jax fell to his knees, but by then Bones and Corbie had gotten between them.

"Calm down," Corbie shouted in Jax's face.

Jax turned and skated to the far side as the refs made their calls. Both Nate and Jax were sent to the penalty box.

It was now four Flyers against six Steers. A two-man advantage for the wrong team.

The arena had gone ballistic, calling insults to the ref for a bad call on Jax.

He could only sit as far from Nate as possible and watch the clock.

If there was a time for the Steers to score, this was it.

And . . . by the time Jax skated out of the penalty box, the score was two to one, Steers leading.

Nothing between him and Nate had changed. If anything, it had just put them more at odds with one another. But Jax would play the game out regardless.

"Let's go," Jax called to Bones just as Corbie passed.

Bones pivoted and passed to Jax, who, two seconds later, sent it back to Bones.

"I'm open!" Nate called.

But Jax ignored the jerk. And Bones knew better, so he passed once again to Jax, and this time he had a split-second window. He sent the puck high net, and it slammed into the top left corner.

The cheers were deafening, but Jax wasn't done yet.

Nate wouldn't even look at him.

And Rocco seemed he was about to put someone, anyone, in a chokehold.

Jax could feel the game getting out of control. By the time the second-period buzzer rang, Corbie had been sent to the penalty box for tripping a Steer.

Jax spoke to no one on the way back to the locker room. He took a quick shower in cold water, then dressed again. His head needed to stay focused. The game was tied up again, and that was unacceptable.

Fifteen minutes later, he was back on the ice, ready for the final period.

No one scored, at least for a while. No one made penalties. They were like circling wolves, and the fans were upset. Booing and yelling for the Flyers to do something, anything.

Finally, Jax passed to Nate, giving him another chance.

Nate pile drove into Rocco, but the beast of a man was ready. Rocco hooked Nate, preventing him from moving forward or backward, and the puck skittered free. Bones was on it in a second, and the ref's whistle blew.

Jax watched as Rocco was ordered to the penalty box.

One man down, and now the Flyers had powerplay advantage for five long minutes.

Nate looked over at Jax, and with the slightest nod, Jax knew they were once again teammates, however briefly.

Rocco would rue the moment he'd caused a penalty, because Nate scored the next goal. Followed by Corbie. A four-to-two lead proved to be too iconic to make a comeback in the third period. And the clock counted down with fans shouting the numbers.

As the entire arena leapt to their feet to celebrate, Jax tugged off his helmet and skated a lap around the ice, holding it high. The screams and yells were nice, but he was only looking for one person. His gaze slid over the women in the row he'd reserved, and then he saw her.

Meg was standing up, clapping, a huge smile on her face. When their gazes connected, she waved, then blew him a kiss.

He nearly lost his footing. Good thing the wall was next to him.

The reporters had already crowded the players' bench, and he knew he'd have to do his duty before he could change and put this game behind him. He skated over to where Sheila, a mainstay reporter for the Flyers, stood waiting in her heeled shoes and fitted business suit.

"Tell us about what's going on between you and Nate Rochester," Sheila said, her eyes wide. "That was some fight between the two of you. Did you forget you're on the same team?"

Jax chuckled, although it sounded hollow. "Things got heated up on all sides," he said. "We had a bit of miscommunication earlier in the game, and well, we got it all worked out in the end." There. That should satisfy her.

"Tell us about Rocco," Sheila continued. "I don't think I've ever seen you guys be so gentlemanlike toward each other."

Now, that was funny, and Jax's laugh was genuine. "I think we've come to an understanding." He shrugged. "We both play different games, but as long as the Flyers come out on top, I couldn't be happier."

It was time to go. He'd answered enough questions. "Thanks, Sheila." A direct look at the camera, and he said, "Thanks, Chicago. This one was for you."

Above the plexiglass some of the fans had lingered to listen in, and they cheered at his last pronouncement.

Sheila faced the camera for her wrap-up, and Jax skated over to where Meg and her grandma had come down the stands toward the bench. He moved out off the ice and across the divider to shake her grandma's hand.

"Nice to meet you, Mrs. Bailey." The woman was tall, not as tall as Meg, but she had that stately presence that reminded him of Meg.

Her eyes crinkled with a smile. "Nice to meet you too, young man," she said, giving his hand a firm shake. "But I'm not sure why you had to get a penalty. You could have let Nate take the fall for that move."

Jax wanted to laugh. He guessed Mrs. Bailey to be in her seventies, yet here she was, taking him to task. "Nate and I have a complicated history. He decided to bring our, uh, personal issues onto the ice."

He could feel Meg's stare, and he thought he'd blown it.

"Well, my Meg tells me that you're setting records left and right."

"Yes, ma'am." He felt gratified to see Meg's cheeks pinken. What else had she told her grandma about him?

"Great game, Jax," Meg said.

He sort of wished they were alone and didn't have all these people around.

Nashelle moved a step down. "Yeah. That was some goal."

He hadn't even realized she was there. It seemed the other employees of Meg's had left.

"Well, it *is* the boy's job," Mrs. Bailey said.

Jax held back a laugh. He hadn't been called *boy* in a long time. Coming from Meg's grandma, it was kind of endearing.

"Sometimes, though, no one scores," Nashelle announced.

Mrs. Bailey turned to look at her fully. "Not when Jax is on their team. Did you watch their last game?"

"A couple of good games doesn't represent the entire season," Nashelle argued.

The two women began to debate, and Jax looked at Meg. Was she going to intervene? Apparently not. She just watched the two women with amusement.

"So what are you doing right now?" Jax asked in a low voice.

"Taking my grandma home," Meg said, centering her gaze on him. The green of her eyes was darker with the black silk blouse she wore. A least she had a coat on tonight. "Then maybe I'll do a little accounting."

"Can it wait?"

"Taking my grandma home?"

"Your accounting."

A smile touched her lips. "Maybe."

"Wanna come to Lucas's birthday gig with me tonight?"

At this, her brows rose. "Where is it?"

"At his house," Jax said. "Totally low-key."

"Low-key with a bunch of hockey players?"

Jax grinned. "We'll stay an hour, tops. Then we can do something more . . . quiet."

Was she blushing? He didn't mind if she was.

"I won't know anyone there," she said. "Except for you. And if I go with you, won't that sort of send a message that we're, uh . . . together?"

"Would that be so bad?"

She was definitely blushing.

"Rocco's coming too. He and Lucas played their first pro year together. And you sort of know Rocco," Jax said. "Nate will be there, but you're not going anywhere near him."

Meg smirked. "I think that would be best for everyone."

"Is that a yes?" Jax couldn't hide the hope in his tone.

"How about I take my grandma home, then I'll let you know about the party?"

Disappointment surged through Jax. This sounded like a delayed letdown.

"I can take Grandma home," Nashelle said.

Both Jax and Meg looked at the woman in surprise.

But Mrs. Bailey didn't seem put off by the idea. Maybe their debate had been healthy?

"Yeah," Nashelle said. "While you two were in your starry-eyed tête-à-tête, I found out that Grandma quilts. I've been dying to learn the Dresden plate quilt block, and she knows how."

Jax had no idea what a Dresden was, but right now he didn't care.

"So go to a party with your boy," Nashelle said in a mischievous tone. "Gran and I will be up late laboring over the art of quilting. Hand over your keys."

Meg opened her mouth and closed it, then looked over at Jax.

"I can get you home. Whenever you want," he added.

She shoved her hands into her coat pockets, but he could see the shift in her eyes. All arguments had faded.

"Okay," she said, pulling out her car keys and handing them to Nashelle.

TWELVE

ROCCO RODE WITH them in Jax's truck, and it was probably a good thing, because the intensity of Jax's gaze on her earlier had made her wish she'd worn lightweight clothing. As it was, Meg shed her coat as soon as she climbed into the truck. Jax's hair was still damp from his shower after the game, and he smelled like freshly showered man.

Rocco sat in the back and kept up the conversation.

Although Jax had been talkative around her grandma and Nashelle, now he'd gone quiet.

Rocco made it his business to quiz Meg about herself, which she didn't mind, but he was really quite the interrogator.

"So you run this boutique, and you're the sole owner?"

"Yes, it's just me," Meg said.

"What got you into the business?" Rocco continued. "Retail is all-consuming. Are you a workaholic?"

"I've always loved fashion and design, and well, it was a natural thing for me after I graduated."

Rocco asked her where she went to school, then Jax interrupted. "Hang on, I've got to get gas." The truck bumped over a curb and pulled into a gas station. "Didn't know I was getting so low. Guess I've been distracted."

"Yeah, you have," Rocco said.

"Shut up." Jax climbed out and shut the door.

Meg looked back at Rocco. Jax hadn't sounded exactly pissed, but he hadn't been pleasant either. "What are you guys talking about?"

"Uh, I shouldn't say," Rocco said. "I'm not getting in the middle of anything."

"What do you mean?"

Rocco sighed. "He's just being possessive."

"About what?" Meg turned more so she could get a full view of Rocco.

He wore a baseball hat turned so the brim was behind his head, which made his face look even more square. He had those dark Italian eyes with amazing eyelashes.

"You."

Meg frowned. "What about me?"

"He's into you, that's all I can say."

A warm flutter erupted low in her belly. "And that makes him grumpy?"

"Ha. No." Rocco leaned forward. "He doesn't like me chatting you up."

This surprised Meg. "But you guys are friends, and we're just being, you know, friendly. Talking like normal people."

"Right." Rocco chuckled. "We know that, because we're normal. But Jax isn't normal. And I am a good-looking guy, right? I mean, you should see the ladies falling down at my feet."

Meg laughed at that, and Rocco joined in, which of course was the exact moment Jax opened the driver's door.

Meg immediately bit back her laugh, and Rocco said, "Got some gas?"

"Yep." Jax didn't look at either of them as he started the engine again.

The next few minutes were silent until Rocco filled that silence with reading texts from the group chat he called The Pit. It sounded like the Northbrook guys were reporting in on their games that night or commenting on each other's. Most of it was ribbing and making fun of each other.

Soon even Jax had cracked a smile.

Meg relaxed a tad, but her pulse had begun to speed up as she thought about all Rocco told her. *He's just being possessive* and *he's into you.* So maybe the attention from Jax hadn't been a strange fluke, and maybe he really did find her interesting.

"Wow," Rocco said, looking up from his phone. "Lucas must make the big bucks."

"Some guys like to show it a little more," Jax said.

And Rocco was right. They'd stopped at the end of a long driveway that led up to a sprawling two-story mansion. Garden lights edged the driveway, lighting the way, but parked cars blocked Jax from driving any further.

Lights blazed from the place, and as soon as Meg opened her door, she could hear the thumping music. She pulled her coat back on and buried her hands in her pockets. She had no idea what to expect, what sort of conversations she'd be a part of, or how she'd be introduced.

"Bones!" Rocco called out to a man who was heading up the porch, about to go inside the house. "How are you, my man?"

"They're friends?" Meg asked Jax. He was back to his brooding self.

"Yeah. Bones played with the Steers before he was traded to the Flyers."

"I wouldn't have guessed, with how they played against

each other tonight."

"Yeah, well, most players are buddies off the ice," Jax said. His hands were shoved deep in his coat pockets too. "There's some crappy stuff that goes on, though."

"What's up, Emerson?" the tall redhead said.

"Hey, Bones," Jax said. "This is Meg."

"Hi." She held out her hand and shook Bones's, which was like grasping the muscled shoulder of an ox.

"Where are you from, Meg?"

"Here."

"Ah, homegrown. Nice, Jax."

"Mind your own business," Jax growled.

Bones and Rocco both laughed.

Meg couldn't help but smile, because this was very, very interesting.

Rocco opened the door to the house and motioned for everyone to go in.

Meg walked in front of Jax and paused in the entryway. The place was massive, and stunning. Lights glowed everywhere, and the ceilings went on forever. Laughter and music came from the great room just beyond.

The guys shed their coats and tossed them on top of a growing pile in a side room off the entrance, so Meg did too. She'd worn her black silk shirt with herringbone-print pants tonight. Her hair was pulled up into a messy knot, and she'd worn dangling silver earrings. Perhaps too dressy for a bunch of athletes in jeans and T-shirts. But she couldn't very well change now.

Bones and Rocco had already walked ahead of them, and Meg turned to Jax. He wore a frown, staring down at his phone.

"Everything okay?"

He looked up as if he'd forgotten she was standing there.

Then his gaze made a slow perusal of her, from her hair to her heeled boots. How did he do that? Make her blush without a word?

"I had a meeting with the coach in the morning," he said. "He wants to push it back until later in the day."

She watched his gray eyes darken. "About your contract?"

"Yeah."

She could practically feel the disappointment and frustration radiating from him. She stepped closer. "It's not like he cancelled it. You'll still know more of what's going on tomorrow, just a few hours later."

"Yeah, you're right." His voice was lower and softer, and his gray eyes moved over her face. He lifted a hand and lifted a tendril of her hair from her cheek. "Maybe we should leave. I don't feel like good company right now."

He was stressed, and she got that. He'd had a great game, and he had a great career, but if he felt he was bought and paid for, no wonder he wasn't in the mood to socialize.

"Let's stay for a few minutes," she said. "We're already here. Tell Lucas happy birthday at least."

He hesitated, then nodded. Together they walked into the main room. A giant big-screen television was on, showing some football game. A table to the side was covered in pizza, chips, and beer. People were everywhere: on the couches, sitting on the floor, perched on stools or chairs. The hockey players, plus plenty of women.

It took a quick glance for Meg to know that she was not like any of the women in their fan jerseys, high ponytails, tight jeans, heavy makeup, and pouty smiles. But she'd just deal with it. After all, she'd practically talked Jax into it.

And they got plenty of attention. Meg would never be able to remember the names of everyone he introduced her to, men and women alike. Most of the guys also had nicknames—it was a thing in sports, she quickly learned.

Nate was across the room, sitting at a card table with a woman on his lap. She had her arms looped around his neck, a hundred percent focused on Nate instead of the card game he was playing. Nate didn't seem to mind, though.

Meg looked away quickly before their gazes could connect. If Jax was fine with being in the same house as Nate, she would be too. Meg refocused on the conversation Jax was having with Corbie—one of his Flyers teammates. They were talking about football, of all things.

Her gaze caught Rocco's from a few feet away. He grinned, then lifted his beer as if to toast her. She smiled and shook her head.

"You should check it out," Corbie said. "It's pretty cool."

"Okay," Jax said.

What was he agreeing to?

She followed the guys up the stairs and walked into a huge arcade room. "Wow."

Corbie laughed. "I could live here all day. Lucas has all the oldies."

Meg looked around. Some of the arcade games she'd played as a kid with her brother. She wandered the room. The lighting was dim, but the arcade games were all plugged in and glowing their iridescent colors, as if she was being beckoned toward them.

"Do we need quarters?" she asked.

"No," Corbie said. "That's the beauty of it." He sat down at a racing game and selected a track. Soon he was driving through a forest on a winding road.

Jax stopped at a pinball machine and pulled back the lever. A metal ball went flying, and he began to work the controls to keep the ball from sinking into a hole.

Meg headed for the Pac-Man machine. She'd been pretty good at it once, years and years ago. She selected one player, then began. The first few rounds were easy and slow, but then the flashing ghosts caught up with her. "Stupid game," she muttered.

"What's stupid?" Jax asked.

She hadn't even noticed him leaving his game and coming to watch her. She glanced at him, then said, "The controller keeps sticking."

His mouth curved. "Let me try."

So she took a step back and folded her arms.

Jax cleared the next level easily, then started on the next one.

"Do you want any drinks?" Corbie said. "I'm going back down."

"I'm good," Jax said.

"Me too," Meg added.

Then they were alone, but Jax was solely focused on capturing tiny cherries and bananas.

"How are you doing it?" she asked. "I swear the controller is off."

"It's an art, I guess," Jax said, glancing over at her with a smile.

It was really good to see him relaxed and smiling.

The board switched to a higher level, one that Meg was pretty sure she'd never reached in her life.

"Here, let me show you," Jax said.

He backed up so she could take the controller, then he moved behind her and rested his hand on top of hers. "It's all in the wrist movement."

"Right," Meg deadpanned.

"I'm serious," Jax said, his warm breath against her neck now, because he was standing rather close.

His large hand completely encompassed hers, and as the cheerful electronic music started up, he moved even closer so that now his chest was pressed against her back. "Relax," he said, "And don't think about the ghosts."

His breath tickled her neck, and she felt like laughing.

But she was trying to make a valiant effort to get through the dots on the screen. Jax was definitely doing all the work, but it was an eye opener to feel how fast and smoothly his hand and wrist moved. He rested his left hand on the other side of her, against the Pac-Man machine, so now she was cocooned between his arms.

Somehow he was still able to play, and play effectively. Meg watched in fascination as the board cleared and the next level loaded. She was breathless. From playing Pac-Man? "I don't think I can handle playing the next level," she said. "My heart rate is going crazy."

"Mine too," Jax's voice rumbled next to her ear.

Her eyes slid shut. She wanted to lean back, feel both of his arms wrap around her. Breathe him in.

The electronic music chimed, signaling that the Pac-Man had been caught by a ghost. Meg opened her eyes. The screen flashed *Game Over*. "What happened?"

"We lost."

But Jax didn't move, didn't pull back, and Meg's heart rate only increased. And she was pretty sure she could feel his heart thumping just as fast.

"Jax, I have to tell you something," she whispered.

"Hmm?" His tone was a delicious rumble.

She rotated slowly. Jax still didn't move back, so when she'd fully turned, they were inches away from each other. The heat of his gaze spread across her skin, pooling in her belly.

"You're the most insecure, secure person I know."

His brows tugged together. "What do you mean?"

"You're an amazing hockey player," she said, resting a hand on his chest, "yet you think the technicalities of a contract can invalidate your career."

His eyes narrowed. "You giving me a pep talk?"

She bit back a smile. "And you have some sort of strange idea that any other guy who talks to me, I suddenly want to date."

"That would be ridiculous."

"Very ridiculous," she said. "Especially since the only guy around here I'm interested in dating is you."

He didn't move for a moment, but his gray eyes said everything that he wasn't saying. When he brought both hands up and cradled her face, she thought she'd melt on the spot. His thumbs dragged along her jaw before he leaned down and pressed his mouth against hers. His kiss was so gentle that she barely felt the warmth of his lips.

She slid both hands up his chest until her fingers spanned his shoulders. That seemed to be all the invitation he needed, because then he kissed her for real.

Meg curled her fingers around his shirt to hold on as he deepened the kiss, tasting her as if he'd been waiting to kiss her for a long time. His kiss was all-encompassing as he explored her mouth, moving his hands behind her neck and into her hair.

She gripped his neck, wanting more, needing more.

He lifted her onto the arcade machine and tugged her legs around his waist. His kisses had set her on fire, and she was pretty sure that not even a dip in an icy river would cool her down.

She moved her fingers into his hair. It had dried, and she'd enjoy messing it up.

Jax's hands wandered down her back, slipping along the silk of her blouse until they anchored over her hips.

"Meghan," he whispered against her mouth.

She could hardly breathe, let alone answer him. "Hmm."

"You're beautiful." He kissed her jaw, then lower, trailing a path of fire along her neck.

She couldn't help tilting her head back and giving in to his touch and the sensations coursing through her.

"You're beautiful too, Jax Emerson."

He chuckled, then his huge hands splayed across her lower back as he drew her tightly against him. "I don't think I've been called that before."

Meg smiled. "Get used to it, because it's true."

THIRTEEN

JAX BREATHED IN Meg's vanilla scent as he pressed a kiss against her collarbone. He was pretty sure that life didn't get better than this. This beautiful woman in his arms, kissing him back and making him feel things he hadn't thought he'd be able to. Not after all the betrayals in his life.

"That tickles," she whispered against his ear.

"What?"

"Your beard."

So he deliberately slid his chin up her neck. Meg squealed, and he began to laugh.

"It's not funny," she said, pushing against his chest, but that did nothing to deter him.

He found her earlobe, and she squirmed against him. "Stop," she said with a laugh. "You're not playing fair."

He lifted his head to gaze into her green eyes, which had darkened to nearly black. "Who says I'm playing at all?"

She bit her lip, her eyes gleaming with amusement as she moved her hands over his shoulders, then down his chest, tracing him as if she was memorizing him. When she reached his stomach, he drew in a breath.

She only smiled and leaned forward, then kissed the base of his throat. "I'm not playing either, Jax."

He closed his eyes. What was it about this woman that made him want to forget everything in his life but her? She pressed another kiss higher on his throat. Yeah, he could get used to this. Then she brushed her fingers against his beard. "You know, I've never kissed a man with a beard before."

"Oh, yeah?" he said. "What do you think?"

"It's nice," she whispered. "But maybe because it's you."

Well, he couldn't let that slide. "Another pep talk?"

She laughed, and then she slipped her hands behind his neck. "Kiss me, Jax Emerson."

He obliged, happily. She was becoming familiar to him now, and it only made him crave her more. Maybe he should find more things that would make her laugh. But when a rendition of the happy birthday song rose from the main level of the house, reality edged its way in.

Meg had heard it too, because she drew away from him, even though he kept her anchored in place. "Someone could find us at any moment."

He rested his forehead against hers. "Let's get out of here then."

"What about your teammates?" Her fingers traced his collar, distracting him further.

"I've done my due diligence, but I'll send Rocco a text." Jax did let her go then. He pulled out his cell and sent Rocco a text. *Mind if Meg and I take off? Can you find a ride back to the hotel?*

Moments later, Rocco's reply came. *No problem. I'll probably call a Lyft with all this drinking going on. Treat her right. I kind of like her more than you.*

Okay, so that last sentence was entirely unnecessary.

"We're good to go," Jax said, refocusing on Meg, who was adjusting her hair.

"Want help?"

"No," she said with a laugh. "You'll just make it worse."

"True." He leaned forward and kissed the underside of her jaw.

"Don't start that again," she teased.

He groaned and pulled back. Then he grasped her hips and helped her down from the arcade. "I think we can officially say we bested Pac-Man."

She swayed toward him, and he pulled her close. "I think you're right," she murmured against his neck.

Cheering sounded downstairs, probably to celebrate a touchdown in the football game. But it reminded Jax that they were far from alone in this house.

They headed down the stairs, and Jax kept ahold of Meg's hand. Everyone could draw their own conclusions; it didn't matter to him. What mattered was that Meg knew he was with *her*, and only her.

It took a few minutes to get through the crowd, and Jax wished Lucas a happy birthday again. Without anyone noticing, they slipped out, grabbed their coats, and headed for the truck. Jax opened the passenger door for Meg, then strode around the front of the truck to the driver's side. A light snow had started, and the clean air felt great. Or maybe he felt great because of what was happening between him and Meg.

He was pretty sure she liked him for *him,* and not because he was some pro athlete worth millions. She'd said it in both words and actions. It seemed that the day he got hit by a car was one of the luckiest days of his life. He climbed into the truck and started it, then looked over at Meg, burrowed in her coat on the other side of the bench.

"Come here," he said. "You're too far."

She unclipped her seatbelt, then moved to the middle portion of the bench.

Jax turned up the heat in the truck, then pulled around the circular driveway. After turning onto the main road, he grasped her hand. "You're cold."

"Getting warmer," she said, leaning her head on his shoulder.

He kissed the top of her head, then rubbed his thumb slowly over her wrist.

"Can I ask you something personal, Jax?"

"Hmm?" He had no problem being an open book with Meg. He felt that comfortable around her.

"What do you do with your money?" Meg asked, lifting her head and looking at him. "I mean, Lucas obviously lives large, and so do most pro athletes. This truck is an older model, and your house is kind of small and modest."

Jax didn't know if he should laugh or be offended. "Is my money why you're dating me?"

Meg placed her hand on his chest, her fingertips brushing the skin above his collar. "That, and you're an incredibly good kisser," she teased.

"You shouldn't say those things when I'm driving."

"Hmm." Meg pressed her lips against his pulse at the base of his neck.

"Not safe," he growled, tugging her hand to his lips.

They were almost to a stoplight, and Jax slowed to a stop. He turned his head and kissed Meg full on the mouth.

She kissed him back, twining her arms around his neck. "You're avoiding my question," she whispered. "And the light's green."

He forced himself to release her and started driving again. She was intoxicating, and he probably needed a cold shower. "If you want to come to my place, I'll show you where my giant paycheck goes."

"Are you trying to trick me into coming over?"

"Never," he said, glancing over to see that she was smiling. "But if it works . . ."

She playfully punched his arm.

"Hey, I'm driving, woman," he said. "You're definitely a hazard."

She sighed. "How much farther?"

"About ten minutes."

It was both the slowest and fastest ten-minute drive of his life. When he pulled into the driveway of his house, he could see what Meg saw. A small, modest home. Nothing compared to Lucas's flashy mansion. But to Jax, this house represented his independence, and possibly his break from his wealthy upbringing.

Of course, his attempts at independence and living a low-key life might all be tainted now. He'd find out soon enough, in the meeting with Coach Lindon tomorrow.

After parking, he walked around and opened Meg's door.

"You're such a gentleman," she quipped, sliding down, right into his arms.

It was really too cold outside to be dallying and kissing her against the side of the truck, but he did anyway.

"Jax," she breathed between kisses. "Do you have a dog?"

Yeah, so Sheriff was going nuts, barking as usual when he heard the truck.

"That's Sheriff," Jax said, reluctantly drawing away from Meg. "Come on, you can meet the loudest watchdog alive. He can probably smell you too."

"Out here?"

"He doesn't miss a thing."

"Where was he when I brought you home from the hospital?" she asked.

"One of my teammates picked him up because I was supposed to be in the hospital for a couple of days."

Jax led Meg to the front door, and as he unlocked it with his key, he called to Sheriff through the door. "Sit, boy."

Sheriff's barking stopped, followed by a pitiful whine that didn't fool Jax. He opened the door and flipped on the interior light.

The Great Dane was still sitting, although his limbs were trembling from holding back his desire to jump all over Jax.

"Good boy," Jax said. "You need to behave yourself, you hear? We have a special guest tonight."

"Oh my gosh, he's huge," Meg said, staring at the gray dog. "How old is he?"

Jax shut the front door, then turned to the dog and crouched before him. Scratching the dog's head, Jax said, "He's three. Wanna say hi?" He looked over at Meg, who was sticking pretty close to the door. "Come on, he's a teddy bear."

When she took a tiny step forward, Jax frowned. "Have you been around dogs much?"

"Not really. My grandma had a cat for a while," she said. "And Nashelle has one of those yappy poodles."

"Okay." Jax straightened and reached for Meg's hand. "He'll want to smell your hand. It's sort of his get-to-know-you, and then from there, you won't have to worry about a thing. He's well trained, and he can understand basic commands. Don't let his size intimidate you."

Meg gave Jax a nervous smile, but he was gratified when she put her hand out for Sheriff to sniff.

"He'd be very obliged if you scratched him behind his ears," Jax said. "You'll have a friend for life."

"Okay," she said with a laugh. She ran tentative fingers lightly over the dog's head, then scratched him. "Oh, he does like it."

Jax chuckled. "Dogs are easy to please. Food, water, a bit of attention."

Sheriff pressed his nose against Meg's leg and closed his eyes.

"I think you have a fan already," Jax said.

Meg seemed to relax more, and that was a good thing in his opinion.

"Ready for bed?" he asked the dog.

Sheriff woofed.

"He answered you," Meg said, her tone surprised.

"Oh, Sheriff loves bedtime," Jax said, giving Meg a wink. "Come on, boy. Let's go find your bed."

Meg followed as Jax walked to the remodeled kitchen. Facing the street was a large bay window. It was Sheriff's favorite place inside the house, so that was where Jax had placed the large dog bed.

Sheriff continued with Jax to the pantry, where Jax flipped on the light and found a treat for the dog. "This is his nightcap," he told Meg.

She stood by the kitchen table, watching it all, her gaze taking in the whole of the room. "It's gorgeous in here," she said. "Did you do the remodeling?"

"Nope," Jax said. "I'm just good at bossing people around." He decided that Meg looked good in his kitchen. Elegant, willowy, with her dark hair and dark eyes, hair escaping her updo and waving against her graceful neck.

Now that he knew what it felt like to touch her and kiss her, it was hard to have any distance between them, no matter how temporary.

Sheriff's impatience made him gobble his treat right from Jax's hand. He chuckled. "Easy, boy. Meg might think I starve you." He patted the dog's head, then said, "Time for bed."

With a drooping head, Sheriff walked into the center of the dog bed.

"Huh," Jax said. "He's pouting. Thinks he's going to miss out on the new visitor, I guess."

Meg ventured closer as Sheriff laid down and rested his chin on his paws. She bent over and scratched the dog again. "What time does he usually go to bed?"

"Whenever I get home," Jax said.

She continued scratching the dog's head, and Sheriff looked mighty pleased.

"You're spoiling him," Jax said. "Now he'll expect you to come over every night. Not that I'd mind."

Meg smirked up at him, then straightened. "He seems kind of lonely."

"It's all just an act," Jax said, moving closer to her and enfolding her hand inside his. "You know, to get the pretty woman to pay attention to him."

Meg turned toward him then.

They were only inches apart, and he sensed her quickening breath. Well, it matched his racing pulse.

"What's your act, Jax?" she said, her fingers trailing up his arm.

"With you, I don't have an act," he said as goosebumps raced across his skin at her touch. "What you see is what you get."

Her mouth curved as her fingers rounded his shoulder, bringing her flush against him. "That's what I like about you," she said in a near whisper. "You're a straight shooter."

He assumed her comment had some history to it. Maybe referring to her ex-boyfriend. And yeah, he could totally relate.

He settled his hands on her hips. Her scent made him want to lean closer and breathe her in. "Have you been checking up on me, ma'am?"

"Maybe."

He leaned down and pressed his mouth at the edge of her jaw. "What did you find?" he murmured.

Her eyes fluttered shut. "That everything you've told me checks out."

"That's good to hear," he said and kissed her right at the edge of her mouth.

He felt her smile.

Sheriff took the opportunity to woof.

"I think someone's jealous," Jax said, then kissed Meg lightly on the mouth. He didn't really want an audience, not even a dog. "Come on, I'm giving you the tour."

FOURTEEN

MEG WALKED HAND in hand with Jax through his house as he flipped on lights. The exterior of the home was certainly modest compared to the remodeled interior. The place was flat-out gorgeous. Not flashy like Lucas's home, but that didn't matter to Meg, and it never would. She hoped Jax hadn't been offended by her comment; she was just genuinely curious.

But as beautiful as the rooms were, the best thing about the tour was Jax's fingers linked with hers. She wasn't sure her feet had touched the ground since that kiss in the arcade room. Okay. So multiple kisses. Jax sure knew what he was doing when he kissed a woman, and thankfully, Meg's research had told her he wasn't a player. Hope had budded in her, and she wondered if this thing with Jax might be the start of something real. Something that wasn't just a fling in his mind or a fluke in hers.

When he led her to his workout room, she paused in the doorway. Several workout machines were positioned throughout the room, including a treadmill and weight machines. Yet covering the walls were black-and-white photos of scenes from what looked like Africa and wells in various stages of construction.

"What's this?" She released Jax's hand and crossed the room to look at the pictures more closely. Some had Jax in them, and it looked like he was either building the wells or overseeing the work crew.

She scanned picture after picture, gazing at the wide smiles of the native villagers, along with a few men and women who were obviously American by their attire. She paused before a picture where Jax was standing to the side of a well, holding the hand of a little kid. Other children had crowded around the well, making silly faces for the photograph.

Meg had to laugh. The enthusiasm and joy coming from the kids was adorable.

She turned to find Jax leaning against the wall next to the door, hands in his pockets.

"Is this your charity or something? Building wells in Africa?"

"Yep."

She stared at him for a second, and when he didn't offer any more information, she continued to scan the pictures on the walls. After she'd completed a full circle, she noticed that the doorframe on the inside of the room was lined with mismatching bricks. Having seen the same type of bricks in the pictures of wells, she knew the bricks meant something. She placed a hand on one of the rough exteriors.

"Did you bring these back from Africa?"

Jax joined her at the doorway. "One for each well completed."

Meg moved her fingers over a few of the bricks, thinking of the thousands of miles that separated Chicago from the hot, dusty African villages where water was the most precious commodity. Her hand paused over one that was almost black.

"That one is from two years ago," Jax said, his voice

rumbling close to her. "We'd just completed the well, and the next morning as we were packing to head home, a fire swept through the village. Because of the well, we had water close at hand, so we were able to save the rest of the huts."

"Wow." Meg turned to look at him.

His gray eyes focused on her. "The bricks of the well might have blackened, but we didn't replace them. It was a symbol, I told them. That their village was strong."

Meg's throat felt tight. "Was everyone okay?"

"Yeah." Jax brushed his fingers against hers, and she linked them together.

"When do you go over there?"

"Every June after the Stanley Cup finals," Jax said. "Some of the guys on the team have gone with me before. Rocco and Clint from Northbrook want to go with me next summer."

Meg nodded. "You're amazing, Jax. *This* is amazing. What got you into digging wells in Africa?"

The edges of his mouth lifted as he scanned the bricks. "My mom, actually. She forwarded me an email link from one of her friends who was sponsoring a fundraiser. My dad was out of town, so she asked me to go with her. It was my first year in the NHL, so I guess I was feeling generous with my new salary. I put in several thousand toward the company. The CEO was so impressed that he came up to me after the dinner and asked me to join his team the following summer."

"And you did?"

He smiled. "Yep. I was hooked. But I found out that the original CEO was a bit shady with the donations, so I started my own outfit."

Meg turned again to the doorframe, still keeping ahold of Jax's hand. "How many wells have you sponsored?"

"Three hundred and five," Jax said. "I've personally worked on about forty of them."

"That's amazing." And it was. Meg had never expected this from Jax . . . not that she didn't think he was capable or compassionate, but it was a far cry from having a collection of sports cars or a luxury cabin. Maybe he had those too. But the bricks in front of her told a different story, a deeper story, of who Jax Emerson really was at his core. And it was beautiful.

She blinked against the burning in her eyes and took a shallow breath that felt shaky. Why she was having this reaction, she didn't know. Maybe it was because the man holding her hand with his rock-steady grasp had lit a flame of hope inside her: that of a new beginning.

"I think this is my favorite room in your house," she said.

He chuckled. "You haven't seen my bedroom yet."

Despite the heat spreading up her neck she looked up at him. "Why's that? More bricks from Africa?"

"Not exactly," he said in a slow voice, his thumb skittering across her wrist. "Maybe we'll save it for another time, though. I'm trying to be a gentleman here."

The heat in his gaze told her that he was definitely making a choice to be valiant. She wanted to kiss him for it. Instead, she took the out that he'd given her, the out that she needed too. Things were really new between them, and she didn't want to get caught up in the physical stuff before she was sure. Before she knew *he* was sure.

"Thanks for showing me your place," she said in a quiet voice. "I love it."

One of his brows lifted, and his eyes flashed with amusement. "You do? Not too . . . dinky?"

"Oh, forget I said anything," she said with a laugh, and she tugged him out of the room by the hand. She needed to get moving, or she'd never leave.

"You need to say goodbye to Sheriff, or he'll feel left out," Jax said.

"Is he still awake?"

"I don't know if he ever truly sleeps," Jax said.

They veered into the kitchen, and Meg scratched the massive dog's head. "Nice to meet you, Sheriff." She could swear the dog understood what she'd said.

"I'll be back soon, Sheriff," Jax told the dog. "Stay in your bed."

"Will he really stay?"

"Until my truck starts up."

Meg smiled. "I don't blame him."

Jax helped her with her coat, his fingers lingering at her neck. She wanted to turn around and wrap her arms around his neck. Pull him in for a kiss.

Jax shrugged into his own coat, then grabbed his cell phone from the entryway table, where he'd left it. Next he typed in a code on a keypad next to the door to disable the alarm, then he opened it.

The cold air sent a shiver through Meg. Jax led her to the driver's side of the truck. "You're sitting by me," he said, and Meg's heart nearly melted.

She gave him the address to her grandma's, and when he put it into his phone, she could see that he had dozens of text messages.

"You're a popular guy," she mused.

He shook his head as he scrolled through a couple of the texts, then shoved the phone into his coat pocket. "It's just The Pit. Rocco outed me."

"With what?"

Jax backed out of his driveway and pulled onto the street before answering her. "Told the guys that I brought a lady friend to Lucas's party."

Meg couldn't read his tone, and she could only see his profile. Obviously Rocco had been referring to her.

127

"Did you want to keep whatever's going on between us a secret?" She had to ask, and maybe it was bold of her, but she wasn't sure how things worked with dating a pro athlete.

Jax glanced over at her. "Why would you say that?"

She looked away from his piercing gaze. Someone had to watch the road. "I don't know. Everything about you is different . . . I'm feeling a bit out of my element here. I mean, you're younger than me, and it was impossible not to notice the women at the party. The type who hang around your teammates. They're gorgeous and outgoing, and they know everything about the game and—"

"Stop," Jax said, grabbing her hand. "Believe me, they're all the same. Like cardboard cutouts. I don't want the same. Can you trust me on this?"

Meg nodded, her throat feeling tight. "Okay." Her voice came out small.

"Rocco can go overboard sometimes with his comments," Jax continued. "I didn't mean for you to think I was upset about the guys knowing about you."

This was good, right?

"I just don't think *you* are their business, except for them to know you're off-limits." Jax made the next turn, but kept ahold of her hand. "It might be a while before I feel like sharing you, though."

She laughed. "What do you mean?"

"You know, like going to those joint couple things?" He slowed at a light and leaned close to her, then pressed his mouth against her temple. "Do you have any obnoxious friends I need to worry about?"

"Not unless you count Nashelle," Meg said.

Jax groaned, and that made her laugh again.

"Yeah, she's unique, but honestly, we've become friends over the months of working together," Meg said. "Especially when the friends I had while dating Blaine drifted to his side. Turns out he's more charming and entertaining than me."

"Let him keep them," Jax said, his voice rumbling against her ear as he pressed another kiss against the edge of her jaw.

"You're kind of sweet, you know that?"

"So I've heard," he said in a dry tone.

When they arrived at her grandma's, several lights inside the house were still on. "Looks like she waited up."

"Does she do that a lot?"

"Um, no," Meg said. "But I've never gone out with a Chicago Flyer before."

Jax chuckled. "Guess I'd better walk you to the doorstep then."

Meg had no doubt he would have anyway. He opened his door, then slid out and extended his hand. When she slid to the ground, he didn't move back, didn't release her hand.

"Do you think she's watching out the window?" he asked, sliding both hands around her back and pulling her toward him. "Because if she is, I'd better kiss you here."

She couldn't stop the smile spreading to her face. "Jax—"

His mouth claimed hers, and she closed her eyes and kissed him back, breathing in everything about him. His scent, his taste, the scruff of his beard, the warmth of his body against hers . . . She pulled him even closer.

Jax might have said that the day of the accident was his lucky day, but she was pretty sure it was *her* lucky day. After she had found out he was okay, of course.

When he drew away, it was all too soon, but she was pretty sure her grandma had heard the truck, so it was also a good thing.

"Good luck tomorrow with your coach," she told Jax. "Call me after?"

His gaze soaked her in. "Okay." Then he pulled her into a fierce hug.

Meg hung onto him. She wished she could help him in some way. When he released her, it was like he'd drawn all her warmth from her. They walked to the porch hand in hand.

"Good night, Meg," he said with glance at the door. Then he leaned down and kissed her cheek.

"Good night, Jax," she whispered back.

He winked, and then he set off down the porch.

She watched him reach his truck before she turned to unlock the door. Finding the door unlocked, she pushed it open.

Sure enough, there was her grandma, sitting at the kitchen table. Eyes as wide as saucers.

"It's late, Grandma," Meg said, shutting the door behind her as the truck pulled away.

"I didn't know if you were coming home or if you had your house key, since you gave your car keys to Nashelle. She said she'd pick you up for work tomorrow since she still has your car."

"Oh, I'm sorry," Meg said. "I should have arranged things better."

"What are your plans with that boy?"

Meg was surprised at this question, but maybe her grandma was overtired. Meg shrugged out of her coat. "I like him, and he seems to like me. But I don't know beyond that."

"I like him too." Grandma stood, using the table to steady herself. "But you need to be careful with your heart. He lives in a different world than you."

"I know," Meg said with a sigh. Even her grandma had noticed. "Thanks for making sure I could get into the house okay."

Grandma patted her arm. "Good night, dear."

Meg should be exhausted, but as she lay in bed, her mind whirled with all that had happened between her and Jax that night. The invitation to the party. Being introduced to his teammates. Their kissing in the arcade. The tour of his house. Her heart rate wouldn't slow, because she realized that she'd allowed her heart to open more than she had thought possible.

FIFTEEN

JAX WORE A suit not because he thought he needed to impress the coach—that was done with goals in the game—but because he was fully prepared to walk away from the team. And a suit would tell Coach Lindon that he meant business.

Yet sitting outside the stadium with his truck idling two minutes before the meeting was supposed to start was an indication that Jax was more nervous than expected.

The anger had long since left, now replaced by a dull dread in his gut.

He wanted to dial back time to last night. When he'd been with Meg and been able to lose himself in her for a short time. She wasn't flighty, she wasn't after his money, she wasn't trying to impress every guy on the team . . . and that was just part of the reason he liked her. She was also quiet and comfortable, and he was more himself with her than he'd been with any other woman.

He'd seen the genuine admiration in her eyes when she'd looked at the pictures of his charity organization. He also loved that she was her own business owner and was independent. She was also compassionate toward her grandma.

One minute. Jax needed to go.

He climbed out of the truck, locked it, and headed into the arena. Coach Lindon's office door was open, but the man was on the phone.

Jax hovered in the hallway, waiting for the call to end, but he couldn't help overhearing the one-sided conversation.

"I don't want him distracted by a lawsuit," Lindon said.

Was the conversation about *him*? Jax moved to the doorway, and Lindon looked up.

"I'll call you back," Lindon said into the phone, then hung up.

"What was that about?" Jax asked, folding his arms.

Coach Lindon was a big guy, though a cancer scare the year before had made him lose some weight rapidly. The guy was a smaller version of his former self, but his blue eyes could still be cold and merciless.

"Have a seat, Jax," Coach said. "I was talking to your dad, so you can follow up with him later."

"Who's my dad suing now?" Jax asked. For Todd Emerson, lawsuits were a monthly thing. He was always buying and selling businesses and using lawsuits to move along the process at a faster clip.

"Discuss it with your dad," Coach said, his tone clipped. Defensive. "What's this meeting about?"

Clearly Coach hadn't missed Jax's attire, because the guy's posture had stiffened and his ice-blue eyes had grown wary.

Jax settled into the seat opposite of Coach. "I thought I'd do you the service of talking to you in person before I get my lawyer involved."

Lindon's eyes narrowed.

Jax rested his folded hands on the desk. "I know about the donations from my dad, and I know that he bribed you to put me on the team. Before you say anything, I'm willing to leave quietly, if only to keep my dad out of jail. And possibly you."

With every sentence, Lindon's face grew redder.

"And," Jax said, holding up a hand to stop Coach from interrupting, "I'm looking to trade before the February deadline. Then, once I'm playing for my new team, I'm going to sue my father to teach him a lesson."

Lindon jumped to his feet. "You're as crazy as your dad."

Jax rose much more slowly. "Just answer me one thing, Lindon. If my dad hadn't flashed his giant wallet in front of your nose, would you have offered me?"

The way the man visibly flinched was Jax's answer, and the only answer he needed. He hadn't expected this meeting to be so short. But now it was over.

Everything else would be handled through lawyers.

Jax shoved back his chair and walked out of the office. He pushed through the arena doors, then pulled out his cell phone. His first call was to Scott. "You're fired."

His second call was to a lawyer he'd worked with off and on. "I need to meet with you as soon as possible."

Griffin's tone was equally brusque. "I have a four o'clock opening if I reschedule a couple of things."

"I'll be there."

The guy worked around the clock, one reason Jax liked him.

His third call went out on his Bluetooth while he was driving back home. "Rocco. Your team looking for a left wing?"

Rocco cut to the chase. "You're looking to trade, Jax?"

"I am," Jax said. "Thought I'd put my feelers out."

"What about your girl in Chicago?" Rocco pressed. "Is she going to follow you?"

"I couldn't say; everything's a bit premature in that department," Jax said. Thoughts of living in a different city as Meg did a weird twist to his insides.

"Uh-huh," Rocco deadpanned. "Mind if I throw it out to The Pit? St. Louis is all shaken up, and Clint's starting to click with everyone on his team."

Jax doubted that. He'd heard enough of Clint's worries to know that it would take several months for most of the teammates to accept a rookie player. "Yeah, sure. I've got some things to get taken care of, but I'm fine with you starting the conversation. You never know who's heard something."

"Okay, man," Rocco said. "And hey, can I ask why you're going to trade?"

Jax drummed his fingers on the steering wheel as he waited at a light. "It's complicated."

Rocco chuckled. "I'm Italian."

"Right." So Jax told Rocco. Almost everything that he'd told Meg. About finding out that his dad had donated the same amount as his contract every year. How he'd been so pissed that he'd walked right in front of a moving car, which Meg had been driving. About his meeting a few minutes ago with Lindon. And how he'd just fired his agent.

Rocco released a low whistle. "When you shake things up, you explode them, man."

"Yeah, well, hopefully my career won't be defined by a contract when all is said and done." Huh. He'd just quoted Meg.

"You're *the* Jax Emerson. You're on your way to the Hall of Fame, and I'm not saying that lightly." Rocco scoffed. "I wish I could have seen Lindon's face. What color was it?"

"Red," Jax said, feeling a smile surface. "Closer to purple maybe."

Rocco laughed.

Jax's smile did break through then.

"Wow, Lindon is the biggest hard-butt in the NHL, yet you made him bluster."

"Yeah." Jax shook his head. "But remember who my dad is."

"We all know who your dad is," Rocco said. "Bless his filthy rich, misguided heart."

"That's one way to put it." Jax pulled into the driveway of his house. More accurately, his parents' house. He'd detoured, and now he didn't know if coming here was a good idea. His dad might not even be at home.

"When are you going to talk to him?"

Jax punched the garage door opener, and one of the three garages opened. Yep. There was his dad's Mercedes. "As soon as I hang up with you."

When Jax hung up with Rocco, he sat for a few moments, fiddling with his phone. Rocco threw out a text to The Pit. *Hey guys, time to rally and help a brother out. Jax is looking to trade. He'll give you details later, but what's the word on the street? Who's looking?*

Declan answered first. *Wow. Sorry, man, if condolences are in order. I'll discreetly ask around.*

Next Clint replied. *Want me to talk to my agent?*

Yes, please, Jax wrote. *Ask him if he wants to rep another hockey player.*

The Pit continued, bouncing back and forth, with everyone chiming in except for Zane. He was probably traveling or catching up on sleep.

Jax pulled up Meg's last text. She'd texted him this morning. *Good luck today.*

He'd replied: *Thanks.*

She'd sent a heart emoji. Which he was now staring at.

He knew that his decision to trade was bigger than

himself. It would affect other things in his life. Things he didn't really want to think about right now.

He climbed out of the truck and headed through the garage.

Clearly his father was getting ready to leave, and even more clearly, he'd be surprised to see Jax. They hadn't exactly spent time around each other recently, and it had been months since he'd been in his parents' home. He knew his mom was at some New York City event and wasn't due home for another day, so in Jax's mind, this was the perfect opportunity to talk to his dad without any interference.

Besides, as disconnected as his mother was with reality in general, Jax didn't think she needed to hear anything that he was about to tell his dad.

His dad was a tall man with deep-brown hair now peppered with gray. His briefcase was on the kitchen counter, and his laptop was open. Impeccably dressed as always, he was typing with one hand while eating a banana with another. Todd Emerson looked up as Jax strode in.

Despite Jax not having walked into this house for months, his dad set down the banana and continued typing with both hands. Ten seconds later, he looked up and folded his arms.

"Lindon called."

Jax perched on the edge of a barstool. "It's all over, sir. What's left to be determined is whether or not I expose you both to the NHL for recruiting infractions and donor violations."

His dad closed the lid of his laptop and slipped it into the briefcase. "No laws were broken. Lindon can distribute any donations as he sees fit. Whether or not he used them as player salaries is entirely up to him, not the NHL. As you'll see in the paperwork I'm having my lawyer send over, everything was done by protocol."

Jax breathed out slowly. "My entire career has been a sham, thanks to you. Why didn't you just put me in band or drama? Save us both this hell?"

His dad snatched a copy of the local newspaper, sitting in the middle of the counter. He flipped to the sports section, then held it up. The headlines read *Powerplayer Jax Emerson Continues Scoring Streak.* "Does this look like a sham? You are a phenomenal player, Jackson. Always have been. When the hockey teams weren't taking a nineteen-year-old seriously, I reached out to Lindon. Like hundreds of parents do for their high school athletes. Sent him some video. Believe me, if Lindon hadn't seen the potential in you, he wouldn't have offered."

This is where his dad didn't get it.

"He offered because you gave him millions of dollars," Jax shot out.

His dad shouldered his bag and came around the counter, his half-eaten banana forgotten. "He took a chance on a high school player. Lindon would have offered the base of a rookie contract, and you would have taken it. But because he had more in the coffers to give you, or any of his other recruits, a better offer, it was just an added bonus. Whether he used it on you or someone else isn't for us to determine."

"You controlled it from the very beginning," Jax said. "You. Not the coach. Not the team. *You.* Just how you like it. Keeping everyone as your puppets."

His dad didn't even flinch. "Sponsors donate all the time, some a lot, some a little. I'm no different than the guy down the street pimping his business with a real estate company banner at the arena."

"Yeah, a banner. With the name of a business on it."

Now his dad's face colored. "What's wrong with putting my money where it will benefit my family the most? My own son? Bring some happiness into his life?"

Jax took a step back. "Do you see me happy, Dad?" He scoffed. "You bribed a coach to make an offer to your son. I've put my heart and soul into this team—beating up my body day after day, night after night—and now I find out that I'm an imposter. That makes me feel like the dirt beneath all of Chicago's feet."

"You're not listening, son—"

"Don't call me *son*." Jax took another step back, his stomach feeling like lead. "This is about *you* and *your* ego. This isn't about me at all. You've screwed around with my life enough. I'm applying for a trade. The farther away from Chicago, the better."

"Jackson, you're making a mistake."

But Jax was done with the conversation. He'd said what he needed to. It was time to leave. Time to move forward in his life. Chicago had nothing left for him. He headed toward the door connecting with the garage.

"Jax!" his father called. "The headlines don't lie! Stats don't lie! You've earned every success on that team, and if anything, you're underpaid."

Jax pulled the door shut. It was all noise. His dad's master manipulation.

Humiliation pounded through him as he climbed into the truck. Without looking at the texts on his phone from The Pit, he turned the phone off. He'd be reporting for tomorrow night's game, but he'd be a shell of himself. All about the mechanics. In and out of the arena. Nothing more.

SIXTEEN

MEG HADN'T HEARD from Jax all day, but she'd thought about calling or texting him about every thirty seconds. The wait was killing her. Of course, her impatience was probably a far cry from what Jax was going through.

It was after 10:00 p.m., and a headache had started as she double-checked the numbers her accountant had sent over. The numbers didn't lie. January 1, she'd be starting the liquidation process. One of her mantras was never to hold sales. The clothing she brought in was top quality, expertly designed, and the value never diminished. But she figured she'd need to get rid of at least half her inventory. The wholesalers offered pennies on the dollar, and Meg hoped she could continue selling through her online shop without too much of a hiccup.

Tomorrow she'd need to tell her employees that she could only pay them through Christmas. She'd also have to call the landlord of her shop and give him the required thirty days' notice.

Meg took a sip of her tea. It had grown cold, and she grimaced. She should go to bed, get some sleep, and maybe she'd be able to think more clearly in the morning. And maybe she'd hear from Jax tomorrow. He had a game. Surely he'd be there. She could grab a ticket and go watch from the nose-bleeds, if only to assure herself that he was okay.

Now she had a plan. That made her feel better, right?

Meg was about to close down her laptop, but she decided to try one more thing. She pulled up Instagram and followed Rocco De Luca. Then she sent him a message. *Hear anything from Jax today? I've been worried.*

Her heart about flipped over when a reply came seconds later.

Not since his coach's meeting. You?

Nothing, she wrote. *I didn't know if I should reach out.*

You should. We're all worried. He hasn't texted since after the meeting. Told McCarthy to set him up a meeting with his agent. Then Jax said he was going to talk to his dad. That was the last I heard. Hours ago.

Meg read through Rocco's message twice. She was both relieved and more worried. Jax had gotten through the coach's meeting, and if he was looking for a new agent, that meant he wasn't quitting hockey completely. Right? She had to believe that was good news for now.

Okay, I'll try calling him. Thanks, Rocco.

Let me know if he's okay.

Will do.

She closed down the app, then took a deep breath. Should she call? Text? Was he home? At a bar? Still with his dad? She pressed CALL on his contact. The call went directly to voicemail, so he must have his phone off. Did he usually turn it off at night? She didn't want to leave a message, but she listened to his deep voice on the message system. *Jax Emerson. Leave a message, and I'll get back to you soon.*

Hearing his voice didn't lessen her worry. Maybe she

should drive by his place, see if he was home. See if there were lights on. No . . .

Meg snatched her purse and keys and cell phone. Then she scrawled a note to her grandma in case she woke up and noticed Meg was gone. On impulse, she loaded a grocery sack with dinner fixings. It could be an excuse if—well, if she needed one.

Her nerves were completely frayed by the time she slowed to a stop in front of Jax's house. His truck was in the driveway, and a faint light glimmered from the living room window, but maybe he always left a light on?

She hated how she didn't know the little things about him.

As she walked up to the porch, she second-guessed herself over and over. But the cold night air was seeping into the jacket she wore, so she either needed to knock or get back into her warm car.

It turned out that knocking wasn't required, because Sheriff started barking, about giving Meg a heart attack. There was no way she could escape undetected now.

The porch light flipped on, and her pulse skyrocketed. She heard Jax's voice telling Sheriff to keep quiet.

Then the door opened, and Jax was standing there. In gym shorts and nothing else.

He'd obviously been working out, if she were to notice the sweat on his skin and the dampness of his hair. But she was trying not to notice, because she was pretty sure her entire face and neck had turned a bright pink.

"Hi." She swallowed.

He didn't say anything for a second, and his gray eyes were completely unreadable.

She should go. Right now. But her body decided to involuntarily shiver.

"Come in," he said. "You look like you're freezing."

She couldn't feel the cold, but she was grateful for the invitation and stepped inside. Would it be rude if she asked him to put on a shirt? To stop looking like he was in some sort of workout equipment photo shoot?

Sheriff nudged her leg, and she'd never been so grateful for a distraction in her life. "Hey, buddy," she said, her voice sounding about an octave higher than it should be.

The front door clicked, which meant that Jax had shut it.

Meg kept her gaze trained on Sheriff. "Sorry, it's kind of late. I tried to call, but . . ."

Why wasn't he saying anything? Helping her out? She peeked up at him. No expression. He'd folded his arms. No hint of whether he was pleased or annoyed that she'd appeared uninvited at his house.

She had to drag her gaze from his sculpted torso and start again. "I called, but I think your phone's off, and I wanted to be sure you're okay." She bit her lip and took another peek. Yep. Arms still folded like he was the mighty Zeus looking over his kingdom or something. "So I asked Rocco if he'd heard anything."

"You talked to Rocco?" Jax unfolded his arms and set his hands on his hips.

Finally, he was speaking. She straightened from her vigorous petting of Sheriff, who promptly whined for more attention. "Well, I messaged him on Instagram. It's not like I have his phone number or anything." Her face was hot again, and she should really stop talking.

Jax stood there, mute again. He was pretty good at letting her trip all over herself.

"So I decided to, uh, check on you." She pushed some hair off her face that had fallen when she'd bent to pet Sheriff. "To see if you're fine." Letting her gaze stray just a tad to his neck, his muscled shoulders, his broad, bare chest. *Heavens.* Could men really have eight-pack abs? It wasn't like she was counting ... "But you look fine. Perfectly fine. Better than fine. And I clearly interrupted your, um, workout. So I'll just leave—"

"What's in the bag?"

She inhaled, exhaled. "Groceries. I thought you might be hungry for dinner. When I have a bad day, my go-to is comfort food."

"You brought groceries to make me dinner?"

Again, she couldn't read his tone. He didn't sound pissed, though. Was that progress? "Yeah." She met his gaze, fully this time. "It will take about thirty minutes. I just have to put the lasagna together and bake it. The meat is already precooked. So thirty minutes, tops."

His gaze flicked over her. "Lasagna, huh?"

She nodded, her pulse thrumming.

Sheriff whined, and Jax ignored him. "I'm not great company right now, Meghan."

"Oh." She tightened her grip on the grocery bag and reached for the doorknob. "No worries. I should go—"

Jax's huge hand closed over hers, stopping her from turning the doorknob. "Stay."

He was a lot closer now, and she could smell his sweat and spice, and everything male about him.

"Are you sure?" she whispered.

"I'd be a fool to turn down your homemade lasagna."

His eyes were lighter now, and that alone gave her hope. Maybe he was going to be okay.

"All right," she said, withdrawing her hand from beneath his. "Do you have a cake pan?"

"There's a bunch of pans in there," he said. "My realtor gifted me a set a while back."

Meg was breathing easier now. Baking she could do. "Great, I'm sure something will work." She moved past him, keeping her gaze averted from his undressed state. "And can you put on a shirt, Jax?"

She headed into the kitchen, so she had no idea what his expression was. Hers, most likely, was a blushing mess. Sheriff trotted after her. A distraction. Good.

"I'm going to shower," Jax said from somewhere behind her. "And I'll see about a shirt."

His tone held amusement, but Meg still didn't dare turn around and check for herself just what he thought about her request.

It didn't take long for her to locate a cake pan and switch the oven to preheat. Jax had disappeared, and Sheriff had become her sole audience. Meg couldn't believe she was standing in Jax's kitchen at ten thirty at night. Making lasagna. Had she lost her mind?

She pulled out her phone and messaged Rocco. *Jax says he's fine.* Well, that wasn't exactly the case, but she wasn't about to divulge anything else. Rocco would probably say something to The Pit, and that would be mortifying, because Jax would see it.

She didn't wait for Rocco's reply but set her phone in her purse. The ringer was on, so she'd hear it if her grandma called. For the next few minutes, she busied herself layering the lasagna, then by the time the oven was preheated, she slipped the pan inside.

Sheriff had grown bored after all, or it really was his bedtime, because he'd lain down in his bed by the window. Chin on his paws, his eyes watching everything.

Next she shredded the half head of lettuce she'd brought and added the other salad ingredients. She didn't have bread on hand for garlic bread, and the bread in Jax's pantry was some sort of sprouted wheat. So they'd skip the bread.

She pulled out the final thing from the grocery bag—a brownie mix. After locating another pan, she found some eggs and oil, then mixed everything with a fork. She heard Jax's footsteps just as she began to pour the batter into the pan.

"Smells good," his voice rumbled next to her.

She didn't turn around, intent on scraping the bowl with the spatula she'd found, one that looked brand new. "Should be ready soon. Sorry I don't have any garlic bread."

His footsteps neared, and her heart rate zoomed.

"What's that?" He was close, really close.

"Brownies," she said. "From a mix, so probably not the best ever."

Jax's fingers brushed her neck, and he moved her hair to the side.

She drew in a breath as goosebumps skittered along her skin. He was right behind her, and his chest pressed against her back as his hands settled at her waist. She was pretty sure she wasn't breathing, and she had to concentrate as she used the spatula to even out the brownie batter.

Jax rested his chin on her shoulder, and his breath warmed her neck.

"Do you even like brownies?" she managed to say without her voice squeaking. "I should have asked."

"I love brownies," he said, his voice low.

Meg's hands stilled. The batter was even enough. "Good to hear."

One of his hands splayed across her hip, while he reached his other hand forward and dragged a finger through the batter. Then he popped the brownie batter into his mouth.

"Hey," she said, slapping at his arm.

He chuckled, and she couldn't help smiling. Then he turned her around to face him. "Want some?"

Thankfully he was wearing a shirt, and she could keep

her wits about her. Although his hands resting on her hips made it sort of hard to keep her thoughts platonic.

"I'll wait until they're baked."

Jax rested his forehead against hers. "You're a wonder, Meghan Bailey."

His hair was damp, and his skin smelled like soap and pine. She looped her arms about his waist, because he hadn't released her yet. "It's just dinner, Jax."

He lifted his head and gazed at her, those gray eyes of his looking past all of her defenses. "It's not just dinner." He raised a hand and moved his fingers along her jaw.

For a moment, she thought he might kiss her, and she wouldn't mind in the least. But then he released her and walked to the bay window, his hands clasped behind his head. The tension had returned to his shoulders.

"I'm here if you want to talk about it," she said. "If not, we can just eat dinner."

Jax didn't answer.

Meg didn't mind. She wasn't going to push him. This was his life, his decision, anyway. She set the brownies in the second oven. Then she scoured for plates, cups, utensils, and napkins. No napkins in sight, so she used paper towels as she set the table.

The lasagna smelled almost done.

"I think I screwed things up," Jax said.

SEVENTEEN

NOT EVEN THE delicious smell of food or the bewitching woman in his kitchen could ease Jax's heart and mind. His conversation with his dad had been playing over and over in his thoughts. The meeting with his lawyer hadn't been as victorious as Jax had hoped. His dad had donated through legitimate channels, and all the paperwork was in place.

There was no concrete proof that the money Todd Emerson had donated had been used directly in Jax's salary.

But Jax had stuck to his resolve of firing his agent, Scott. About an hour ago, he'd spoken with the McCarthy brothers' agent. Jax was impressed with Marcus, and Jax knew that signing with the new agent would be a step forward in his career.

But after that, things got murky.

The dishes clinked behind him as Meg set the table. He should be helping, but nothing about him was functioning normally. Even Sheriff had kept his distance. The dog was sitting in his bed, head down, as Jax stared into the darkness out the bay window. The only thing he could see was his own reflection gazing darkly back at him.

Meg wasn't pushing him for answers, which he appreciated. Things were far from sorted out in his own mind, so how could he explain to someone else? She hadn't commented when he'd said he thought he'd screwed things up. Just continued setting the table.

A buzzer went off, and he turned. Apparently his oven had a timer. One he'd never used. He watched Meg use one of his kitchen towels to pull out the steaming pan of lasagna from the oven.

He crossed over and shut the oven door, then turned it off. She had the brownies in the second oven, something else he'd never used.

Meg looked at him over her shoulder. "We can start on the salad. The lasagna needs to cool for a few minutes before it can be cut."

"Okay," Jax said.

Her gaze held his, and he found that he was enjoying the flush of pink on her cheeks—likely from the heat of the lasagna pan. She was dressed more casually than he'd ever seen her. Her black jeans hugged her legs. Her formfitting V-neck shirt was a dark green, making her eyes look even greener.

She wore no makeup and no jewelry, and he liked that she didn't feel like she had to get all fancy for him.

"I'll sit," he said. "But you first, ma'am."

Her brows lifted, and a smile stole onto her face. She moved toward him and took the chair he'd offered. Then he sat in his own chair.

"What's this?" he asked, picking up a mason jar full of something white.

"Salad dressing. Homemade."

He unscrewed the lid. "I can't remember the last time I had homemade dressing." After Meg took some salad, he piled

150

a bunch onto his plate. Then he drizzled the dressing across the greens. His grumbling stomach told him it had been neglected for far too long.

It took only one bite for Jax to consider proposing to Meg on the spot. "Wow," he said, then took another bite, and another. "You're spoiling me for all future salads."

Meg finished long before he was done eating his second helping of salad. When he looked up, she was gazing at him, her chin resting on her propped hand.

"It's amazing," he said. "Clearly."

She laughed, and he felt some of his cold insides thaw. Whatever had possessed Meg to come over tonight, he was grateful for it.

"I think the lasagna should be done." She popped up from her chair, and in a moment she'd returned, carrying the entire pan to the table. "Seeing how much you're eating, I decided that the pan belongs on the table."

"I think you're right."

She remained standing as she cut a large square and set it on a fresh plate for him, then cut a smaller square for herself. Much smaller.

"Not hungry?" he asked.

"I don't usually eat this late," she said, sitting again.

"Me neither, but you don't see me turning anything down."

She smiled and picked up her fork. "Dig in, Jax, and be prepared to be amazed."

"I'm already there." He dug in, not having to be asked twice. The combination of melted cheese, hot pasta, and spicy meat made his eyes slide shut as he chewed. When he opened them again, Meg was holding back a laugh.

"That expression was worth every second of preparation."

Jax reached for the water glass and took a long swallow. Then he used a paper towel to wipe his mouth. "Come here," he said.

Her brows tugged together. "What are you talking about?"

He grasped the edge of her chair and pulled it closer to him. Then he leaned in and kissed her.

Her eyelids fluttered shut, and she rested a hand against the pulse of his neck as she welcomed his kiss. Her scent of vanilla and cinnamon wrapped around him. "You smell good," he whispered against her mouth.

She smiled, then moved her hand lower and pushed against his chest. "Jax, eat." After tugging her chair back into place, she pointed her fork at his plate of lasagna. "It's warm."

"Oh, so you're one of *those* women."

Meg laughed. "I guess so. Do you have a problem with that?"

"If you'd come closer," he drawled, "I'd prove that I don't." Her blush was gratifying.

She speared a piece of lasagna and popped it into her mouth. He did the same, but not before he tugged her chair a couple of inches closer. This time she didn't move it back into place.

The food, the teasing, the presence of Meg in his house had begun to ease the tightness of his chest. But it didn't ease the situation he'd found himself in. He took another bite. The perfect blend of tastes was like heaven, and he wanted to delay the inevitable just a bit longer. When he told Meg about his various meetings and conversations that day, the impossibility would crowd back in.

"This is fantastic," he said after another bite. "You should market and sell this. You'd be richer than Lucas."

Meg's eyes narrowed. "Yeah, then it wouldn't be home-made anymore. Besides, it wouldn't taste as good packaged, frozen, and reheated."

"You're probably right." He finished off the lasagna she'd served him and went for a second helping.

Meg had finished her small portion, and when she began to clear the table, he grasped her arm to stop her. "I'm cleaning up."

"It's fine. You finish eating, and I can get a head start."

He didn't let go of her arm, not yet. "Are you in a hurry?"

She blinked. "No."

"Then sit," he said. "I'm cleaning up."

"Okay," she said, her eyes sparking with amusement.

"Tell me about your day," he said.

While she talked about some of the customers she'd encountered that day, he continued eating.

"You really want to hear about this stuff?" she asked after a few moments.

He set his fork down. "I do."

"This isn't one of those things where I talk and you fall asleep, is it?"

Jax drank the rest of his water. "No," he said, rising to refill his glass. "First of all, I'm not fresh out of the hospital, and I still haven't had the brownies."

"Oh!" Meg jumped up. "I forgot to set the timer." She rushed to the oven and cracked open the door.

Jax met her there and flipped on the light. "You can see inside."

"I know, but I want to smell it too."

"What do you think?"

"They're perfect." She moved past him to grab the kitchen towel. Then she took the brownies out and set them atop the stove.

Jax began to clear the table, then he rinsed off the dishes and set them in the dishwasher. Once he had them loaded, and the pan of leftover lasagna in the fridge, he bent to study the buttons on the dishwasher. "I've never even used this thing. Never had enough dishes to worry about it."

Meg laughed. "Are you serious?" She joined him at the dishwasher. "First you need to put in dishwasher detergent. Do you have any?"

"Sure, I got some a couple of years ago."

Meg smirked and opened the cupboard beneath the sink, then she nudged him to the side with her hip.

"Hey," he said, capturing her around the waist. He pulled her close and kissed her neck.

She laughed and wriggled away from him. "You're a horrible staller."

"I'm not stalling."

"You are." She put the detergent pod into a miniature compartment at the base of the dishwasher, then she closed the door. "Here, look."

He moved closer, his arms sliding around her again.

"Focus, Jax."

He nuzzled her ear and inhaled the sweet scent of her. She elbowed him playfully, but he didn't budge.

"Okay, it's running."

He lifted his head. "It is? I can't hear anything."

"You got the top-of-the-line. Hardly any sound."

Jax frowned. "How do I know that it's on, then?"

She pointed to a red light on the dishwasher. "This means it's on. It will turn off when the cycle is finished."

"Okay," he murmured, pressing his mouth against her jaw. "Sounds good."

She turned slowly in his arms until their bodies were flush and her arms were looped around his neck.

This was better, Jax decided. He ran his hands slowly up her back, and her smile grew. "What?" he whispered.

"You," she whispered back.

"What about me?"

"You're looking better," she said. "My grandma was right."

He raised his brows. "About . . ."

"A well-fed man is a happy man."

"Hmm." He brought his hands around to cradle her face. "Partly true."

"What's the other part?"

"You. I'm happy because you're here."

She laughed, and he was done waiting. He leaned down and kissed her. Her fingers threaded through his hair as she kissed him back. Her taste, her touch, her body pressing against his made his heart hammer. He rotated so that his back was against the counter, and he drew her closer, kissing her deeper, more deliberately. Memorizing her. Things were going from zero to sixty in just a couple of minutes.

He needed to slow it down. "Meghan."

She sighed. "I know."

Inch by inch, they disentangled from each other, and Jax slid his hand down her arm, then linked their fingers. "Come on," he said, leading her out of the kitchen.

She followed as they walked down the hallway to the office, which overlooked the frozen backyard. He released her hand, then turned on the two lamps and flipped on the gas fireplace. The office was more of a suite, with a large desk, a leather chair behind the desk, several bookcases, and a leather loveseat by a coffee table.

He crossed to one of the floor-to-ceiling bookcases and pulled out a photo album.

After setting it on the coffee table in front of the couch,

he sat down and patted the cushion next to him. When Meg had sat by him, he said, "My mom made this for me last year as a Christmas gift. It's probably the first homemade thing she's ever done for me."

"A baby photo album?"

"Not quite," Jax said, turning to the first page. "More like hockey memories."

"Oh wow, that's you?" Meg said, pointing to the picture of him when he was about six and had put on hockey skates for the first time.

"Yeah." Jax wasn't looking at himself, though. He was looking at the man standing beside him—his father—and the proud smile upon his face. Jax's mom had been behind the camera that day, and he clearly remembered her making them pose for more than one picture.

Jax had shed a few tears that day as he learned that falling on the ice hurt, caused bruises, and took his breath away. But that night, after his first try on the ice, he remembered his dad coming into his bedroom and handing over a magazine with a picture of a top hockey player on the cover.

"He started skating when he was six years old too," his dad had said. "Now he's a pro hockey player in the hall of fame. If you stick with something like he did, you could be anything you want."

The gleam in his dad's eyes had stoked a fire in Jax's chest that night. A fire that had carried him through months and years of practices and games. And he knew it was still there. Despite the icy disappointment that had been crushing him lately.

EIGHTEEN

MEG HADN'T EXPECTED Jax to get so personal with his childhood and, frankly, with his entire life tonight. The photo album showed pictures from his youngest experiences in hockey up to his club days with the Northbrook Hockey Elite team. He paused on a picture of him at about ten years old, holding a giant trophy, surrounded by his parents, and it made her smile. His mom was a gorgeous redhead.

"So that's where the red comes from," she said, tapping the picture of him with his parents.

"Yeah." Jax's arm brushed hers. "What do you think?"

"About red hair?" she asked, looking up to find his steady gray eyes on her. She rested her hand on his neck, her fingers brushing the edge of his beard. "It's okay, I guess."

One side of his mouth lifted, and she leaned close enough to whisper in his ear. "It looks good on you, Jax Emerson."

He stilled, and she could swear she heard his heart thumping. Her own pulse was racing a mile a minute, and she knew that she should probably stop touching him if she wanted to see the rest of the album.

She pulled away and flipped the next page. "There's Rocco." It was a younger version of him, but he was still intimidating even as a teenager. All the guys were, including Jax, although she'd seen a much softer side of him now.

His vulnerability was both surprising and endearing.

"Yeah, he was a beast even back then," Jax said, resting his hand on her back. "You'll have to meet the other guys."

Meg's heart skipped a beat at how casually Jax had said that, as if . . . they were already a couple, and he wanted her to meet his friends. Well, he had taken her to that team party.

"Which ones went pro?" she asked.

"There were five of us called up soon after club. Some played in the minor leagues, but we're all pro now." He leaned forward, bringing them closer together, and pointed to a picture of a tall guy with crooked grin. "That's Clint McCarthy. He got injured his senior year in high school, so he wasn't recruited. Did some college, then he went into the Marines for four years. When he returned, he ended up playing in the minors. Last month he was offered by the St. Louis Hawks. We play them tomorrow night."

"Oh wow," Meg said. "Who's that? He looks like he's going to kill someone."

Jax chuckled. "Zamboni? Yeah, he doesn't mess around when it comes to hockey."

"His name is seriously Zamboni?"

"Nah," Jax said. "Zane Winchester. Plays for the Tennessee Hounds. Spoiled with all that nice weather. Although we can't give him too much crap, since he's a single dad now and he's gone through some rough things."

Meg nodded. "What about this guy?" She pointed to an olive-skinned, dark-haired man.

"Declan Rivera," Jax said, his fingers skimming along her back. "He was the most recruited of our group. Had offers from all over the country. Dice has broken a million records with the Denver Chargers."

"*Dice*, huh?" She peeked up at Jax. "I'm sure there's a story there."

He winked. "Yep."

That wink zoomed straight to her heart. This was nice—Meg sitting next to Jax as he talked to her, his low voice rumbling in the cozy room.

"Who's the other guy that was recruited pro?"

"Trane Jones." Jax pointed at a guy on the far left. "He's as tough as they come. During his teen years, he was about a heartbeat away from being homeless. My dad paid all of his club fees."

Meg heard the sigh in his voice.

"It was a wise investment, of course," Jax said. "Coach Fenwick was like a dad to him, and he taught Trane to be a man on the right side of the law. I'll never forget the day he punched Zamboni in the face and laid him flat on the ice. Zamboni had called him a beggar."

"Wow, did the coach get mad?" Meg said.

"Fenwick didn't have to," Jax said. "That day, Trane earned both respect from all of us and his nickname Diesel."

"Did they ever become friends?"

"Friends isn't exactly what I would have ever called them," Jax said. "But they were teammates, and they worked together. Sometimes that's more important." He flipped another page in the photo album, to a picture where Jax was sitting at a table—obviously signing day. And behind him were both his parents, smiling for the camera. The pride in their eyes was immense.

"Your mom is really beautiful," Meg said. "She looks happy too."

"Those were the good days," Jax said in a quiet voice. "Things have been strained between us for a while."

She heard the disappointment in his voice. "I'm sorry."

She really had no advice; she'd never even met the woman. Besides, both of Jax's parents seemed to live in an entirely different world than she did, so what advice could she offer?

"Well," Jax said, moving his hand from her back and snapping the album closed. "She was disappointed that I broke things off with Lacy."

Meg frowned. "Even after how she let your dad bribe her?"

He gave a short nod, then leaned back on the couch and folded his arms. "Here's the thing. I talked to my dad earlier today, and he was adamant that he donated through completely legal means. So I had my lawyer pull all the accounting reports this afternoon, and it turns out that my dad's donations were legit." He scrubbed a hand through his hair. "Which doesn't really make my decision easier."

Meg felt the breath leave her. "What decision?"

"To accept a trade before the February deadline."

Meg tried not to react. So he was going to leave the Flyers, leave Chicago? "Where will you go?" Her voice sounded faint.

"I don't know yet," he said, his gaze slipping away. "Could be anywhere. I had a phone call with Clint McCarthy's agent, because I fired mine today. Marcus is really hopeful that I'll get a strong contract. Probably five years minimum."

She nodded, although her mind was reeling with all of this information.

"I realize, now that I know what my dad did was legal, he was doing what he thought was best," Jax said. "Although I still think it's messed up. At least I'll not be suing him now."

She didn't know what to say. It was good he wasn't going to sue his own father, but did he really have to leave Chicago to prove a point? "What did your coach say in the meeting?"

He blew out a breath. "Lindon didn't deny anything, but he didn't exactly tell me he wanted me to stay on the team."

Meg couldn't understand how any coach would want to let Jax go. His career had been amazing. Was *still* amazing. She swallowed against the growing lump in her throat. "So staying with the Flyers is completely out?"

"Looks like it."

Their gazes connected, and she saw both pain and resolve in his gray eyes.

She rested her hand lightly on his knee. "This morning's news talked about how last night was the first night in years that the Flyers arena had been completely sold out. Said it was because everyone wanted to see Jax Emerson score."

Jax didn't move for a second, didn't answer. Then he unfolded his arms and placed his hand over hers. "You sound like my dad."

Meg bit her lip. Was this a good thing? "I've never met your dad, so I can't really speak for him, but Chicago would really miss you."

Jax's gaze dropped to their enfolded hands.

"That's what my mom said."

"You talked to her too?"

"Yeah. She called me from the airport. She'll be at tomorrow night's game." Jax shifted forward and snaked his arms around her, pulling her against him.

Meg wrapped her arms about his torso and closed her eyes.

Jax rested his chin on top of her head. "You should meet her."

Her heart thumped hard. "Your mom?"

"And my dad." He slid his fingers up her arm, then he moved her hair aside and rested his hand on her shoulder.

Goosebumps skittered across her skin at his touch. She didn't want him to leave Chicago. Didn't want him to trade. But she was in no position to ask. They'd barely started dating.

So what if she could see herself falling in love with him? She knew from experience that relationships could be very, very complicated, despite anyone's best intentions.

She was having a hard time imagining Chicago without Jax Emerson. For the Flyers' sake and for hers. And she didn't expect Jax to invite her along. That would be crazy. Crazy serious.

Meg tried to erase her mind from the worries of tomorrow and just let herself be nestled against Jax, with his arms around her. She loved that he'd told her what had happened that day, and she loved that the more they were together, the more he shared with her.

"Do you want to come to my game tomorrow night?"

She opened her eyes, realizing she'd started to drift. Work would be busy since she had to finish up inventory while staying open too, but she'd be foolish to turn down Jax. "Yeah, I can come."

"How many tickets do you want?"

She bit her lip. "Is four too much again?"

"No problem," he said. His fingers were playing with her hair, and the feel of his body against hers was doing all sorts of crazy things to her pulse.

She should go, like right now.

"Do you have a busy day tomorrow?" he asked.

"Inventory, mostly." She didn't want to get into the fact that she was having an employee meeting tomorrow to deliver bad news. "I'm making some changes to the operations, and we need to do some holiday decorating."

"You don't start after Halloween like most stores?"

"No, we don't really do sales at the boutique, so we keep holiday stuff to a minimum," she said. "I mean, I'm buying select clothing, and discounting it only cheapens the rest of our inventory. Plus the women who shop at the boutique aren't necessarily bargain hunters."

"Ah. My mom might like your place."

"She's welcome anytime," Meg said. "I'll give her the owner's discount."

"Like you gave me a discount?"

Meg smiled. "Sorry about that." She drew away enough to meet his gaze. His eyelids were half shut. "Next time you come in, remind me."

"It's fine," he said, the edges of his mouth lifting. "I mean, you did say that scarf was handwoven silk. Worth every penny. I should have bought a dozen."

"Hey." She slapped his chest, and he laughed. Warmth soared through her at the sound of his laughter.

Her ringing phone coming from the kitchen made Meg scoot off the couch. "Um, that might be my grandma. Hang on."

She hurried to the kitchen and dug her phone out of her purse. It had stopped ringing, but the missed call was from Nashelle. A text came in just then.

Can't make the meeting so early, Nashelle texted. *Bubba's been sick, so I'm taking him into the vet.*

Bubba was Nashelle's dog.

Okay, keep me posted. Meg would probably have to tell the employees separately then, and that was fine. It had to be done sooner than later so they could start looking for other jobs.

"Everything all right?" Jax asked, coming into the kitchen.

"Yeah." Meg glanced at him. He looked adorably rumpled, and she wanted to walk into his arms and stay longer, but she needed to get back to reality. "It was Nashelle." She told him about Nashelle's text as Jax moved closer to her.

As his hands slid around her waist, she said, "I should probably get going. You have a game, and I've got a full day tomorrow."

"Okay." He leaned his forehead against hers and closed his eyes. "Thanks for coming over, Meghan."

"You're welcome." She moved her hands over his shoulders, her fingers following the contours.

"And thanks for dinner. It was amazing."

She smiled and moved her hands behind his neck. "You're welcome, again."

His lips brushed hers. "And thanks for listening to my drama."

"Anytime," she whispered. And she meant it.

Jax kissed her again, slowly, like he didn't want to rush his goodbye. She didn't mind his long goodbye in the least.

NINETEEN

JAX SKATED ABOUT the rink, hockey stick in hand, as the music blared throughout the arena during warmups. They were playing the St. Louis Hawks tonight, and Jax had been watching their film most of the afternoon. Clint McCarthy, or Fido as everyone was calling him, was on fire.

He skated like his feet were in flames, and his passing was dead-on.

Jax would have to either stop him or get around him. And that might not be pretty.

The announcer's voice boomed as the music quieted, and the Flyers lined up for introductions. That gave Jax the chance to search out the crowd. His dad was in his usual box, along with his mom. It would be good to see her again. He'd been more than surprised at her phone call yesterday. She'd obviously talked to his dad, and it seemed in this one matter, they were on the same page and agreed he should stay in Chicago.

But Jax knew he needed a clean break, a new start, if he was ever to have his own life.

He searched out the area where Marcus would be sitting. His new agent was in his seat, reading through the media guide. Next Jax scanned the area where he'd reserved tickets for Meg and whomever she brought along with her. There was Nashelle, all in black, and . . . no grandma. Then he saw Meg. Walking down the aisle. Wearing his jersey number. Eleven.

Jax couldn't have stopped the grin that spread across his face.

"They just announced your name, dude," Bones said, shoving his shoulder.

Jax pushed off onto the ice and raised his hockey stick to the cheers from the fans. But his gaze was still trained on Meg. Her gaze connected with his, and she stopped in the aisle and started to clap.

He winked, and he was pretty sure she blushed. The distance made it hard to tell for sure, but he didn't care. She was wearing his number, and he knew it meant something.

"She's looking good," Nate said as Jax skated past him and took his place in the lineup.

Jax was too happy to be pissed about the comment.

And then the music rumbled to life again, and Jax returned to the players' bench to grab his helmet and strap it on. He glanced at Lindon. The coach hadn't spoken a direct word to him all night.

But now Lindon moved toward Jax. "The arena's sold out again. Nice job, Emerson."

The coach turned away to talk to someone else, and for a moment, Jax didn't move. He was stunned. Had Lindon just said that?

Jax exhaled, then skated into position, lining up across from Moose on the Hawks' team. A beast of a guy, but Jax had bested him over the years. No big deal. His gaze was on the tall center. Clint McCarthy.

The whistle blew, and Jax backtracked as Clint took first control over the puck and passed to Moose.

Jax intercepted the puck, and the arena went wild. Moose

166

was on him in a second, edging him out, but Jax threw an elbow. The ref blew a whistle, but Jax didn't mind; he'd made his point. No penalty box, since the elbowing hadn't caused an injury.

"Nice one, Emerson," Corbie said, skating past.

Not everyone found it impressive, because as soon as the puck was live again, Moose came barreling toward Jax. He dodged the behemoth and ran right into Clint. The timing was impeccable, because Clint had just intercepted a pass between Nate and Roof.

Jax took control, pivoting and barreling past the Hawks, straight toward their goal.

What he didn't see was Clint, who plowed into him from the side. Jax veered off course, control of the puck gone. The arena groaned their disappointment and screamed for a foul. But it had been a clean interception, and Jax righted himself and turned around.

Clint had the puck again, and Jax was too far away to do anything about it. Hopefully he could catch the rebound shot if Lucas did his job on goal.

Lucas failed. Clint scored.

"And the Hawks score first!" the announcer yelled to a booing arena.

Clint's grin was about a mile wide as he skated back to center position, and Jax had to hand it to the guy. The shot had been beautiful.

And Moose still had his number. The guy was practically frothing at the mouth.

Jax squared his shoulders as the puck dropped, then he pushed off at a dead power move straight across Moose's path. Jax clipped the guy's skate with his hockey stick, and Moose nearly tripped. Jax ignored it and cornered Clint against the plexiglass.

167

"Welcome back to Chicago," Jax ground out as he stole the puck.

"Welcome to your team losing," Clint said, stealing the puck right back.

"Corbie!" Jax shouted. In a single move, he had control of the puck again and blindly passed it, hoping that Corbie was there.

He was.

Jax escaped Clint and skated for the goal just as Corbie returned the pass. Jax deflected the puck and shot into the deep corner, a centimeter past the Hawks' goalie's left skate.

Music blared as the fans screamed. *Jax! Jax! Jax!*

Jax's heart and head were both pounding furiously.

One to one.

Time to turn up the heat.

He circled back to position, his gaze connecting with Bones. They didn't need to say anything to know that both were on the same page. They had to keep the momentum, no matter the cost.

Nate decided not to be left out of the equation.

Clint won the puck and drove it to the Flyers' goal, but Lucas was ready and blocked the shot.

Nate passed to Corbie, who passed to Bones, and Jax skated with Bones into Hawks territory.

Someone clipped him, but he recovered in time for Bones to shoot on goal. The Hawks deflected, but Jax was right there with a second shot. He punched the puck high, so that it sailed right under the goalie's arm and into the net.

The arena turned into a stampede. Jax had just scored twice in eight minutes.

He turned to raise his hockey stick in celebration when Moose checked him from behind. Jax went to his knees, sliding across the ice.

The whistles blew, the crowd screamed, and Moose went to the penalty box.

"You okay?" Corbie said, gripping Jax's arm.

"Yeah." Jax moved to his feet and circled the ice, trying to shake the blurred vision. It was clearing, and that was good. Coach stepped out onto the ice, but Jax waved him off.

He lifted his hockey stick to show the fans that he was fine, and they cheered and clapped. His gaze landed on Meg, who was standing, her hands over her mouth.

I'm fine, he wanted to tell her. *And we're going to win this game.* Moose was out for five minutes, and Jax planned to take advantage of it.

The Hawks scored in the second period, but the Flyers scored twice more in the third. One by Corbie and the final one by Jax.

The arena erupted on the final goal, and Jax glanced over at Lindon. He stood with his hands on his hips and gave Jax an approving nod.

Jax might be trading teams, but he'd go out in style.

As the final seconds of period three ticked down, the fans shouted along with the countdown numbers. Then the final buzzer rang, and Jax took a victory lap with his team. He was happy with the recognition, and his heart still pounded from the exertion, but right now, he wanted to be with Meg and Meg only.

Before heading to the team bench, Jax paused by their opponents' bench, where the Hawks were vacating the space.

"Nice game, kid," Jax told Clint.

Clint turned, a half smile on his face. He clasped hands with Jax. "You're the legend, man. You're gonna have every team clamoring for you."

"Yeah, well, we'll see," Jax said. "You hanging with Marcus tonight?"

"Yep." Clint pulled off his helmet. "My brother's going to come too—he's off-season. Wanna join us?"

"I might stop in. Text me the details."

Clint laughed. "You got your woman on your mind, don't you?"

"Maybe."

"Jax Emerson, mind if I ask you a few questions?"

He recognized Sheila's voice immediately, and he turned around.

"Sure thing, Sheila."

She smiled, her lipsticked mouth stretching wide. "How about that game, huh? Did you at any point think the Flyers were going to lose?"

Jax glanced about the arena. The place wasn't clearing out anytime soon. People were sticking around, talking and celebrating. More reporters than ever crowded the ice, interviewing other Flyers players. Jax looked into the camera. "The Hawks are a great team, and they have some of the strongest players in the league. But no, I didn't think we were going to lose."

Sheila laughed a chirpy laugh. "Your three goals certainly helped."

"Every point helps." Jax shrugged. "It doesn't matter much who makes them, just that they're made."

"I don't know about that, Mr. Emerson," Sheila said, her blue eyes sparkling. "You're scoring points that seem impossible for other players to score."

Jax rubbed the back of his neck. "Yeah, well, I'm just happy to see so many of the fine people of Chicago out here tonight."

"Tell us about Clint McCarthy," Sheila continued, her full smile back. "He's a Northbrook alumnus. How is it playing against your old teammate?"

"Clint's a great player, and he's well on his way to a stellar career," Jax said.

"What about the rumblings between the two of you at the beginning of the game?"

"No rumblings," Jax said. "Just hockey." He directed his gaze again into the camera. "Thank you for all your many years of support, folks. Have a good night."

The interview was over; Jax had other things to get to tonight.

"Thanks, Sheila," he said, then turned and headed into the players' box without waiting for her to come up with more stalling questions.

His parents were coming down toward him, and he nodded his acknowledgment, then looked for Meg. She was still in her seat, talking to Nashelle. *Look over here,* he willed. A few seconds later, she glanced over at him, and he motioned for her to come down. He couldn't very well go up the steps in all his gear. He'd be mobbed for signatures.

Meg's smile was quick, and she nodded. Then she said something to Nashelle.

Soon she was heading down as well.

He turned his attention back to his parents. "Mom," he said as Gina Emerson reached him. Her red hair was pulled into an elegant twist, and she wore a pale-ivory suit that made her look like she'd stepped out of a board room meeting.

"Jax, honey," his mom said. "I'm so happy to see you. You did wonderful tonight."

Jax knew his mom wouldn't hug him when he was covered in hockey sweat, so he leaned down and kissed her powdered cheek.

"Great game, son," his dad said.

Jax flicked his gaze to his dad, who stood behind his mom. The man was wearing a designer suit as usual. "Thanks," Jax said. Simple, short. Despite all that his lawyer had found, the information still sat like a stone in Jax's gut. If his mom hadn't been here, Jax probably would have gone straight to the locker room.

But Meg was here too.

"Mom, Dad, I want you to meet someone."

The introduction would be completely out of the blue for his parents, but that's how Jax wanted it. He didn't want his mom or his dad looking up everything on Meg. He wouldn't put a background check past his dad.

"Oh?" His mom smiled, not a wrinkle on her carefully botoxed face.

"Hey," Jax said, looking past his parents to Meg. "Come here." He wanted to scoop her up in his arms and tell her she looked adorable in his jersey. But he kept things formal, with his parents both looking at Meg with interest.

She gave him a nervous smile, and he grasped her hand. She held onto him pretty tightly, and he squeezed her to give her reassurance.

"Mom and Dad, I'd like you to meet Meghan Bailey," Jax said. "We've been dating for a few weeks." He looked down at Meg. "These are my parents, Todd and Gina Emerson."

Still clinging to his hand, Meg extended her right hand. "Nice to meet you both."

His mom stepped forward and grasped Meg's shoulders. "Oh, it's wonderful to meet you too." Then his mom air-kissed Meg's cheek.

Meg only smiled.

Next his dad stepped forward. His brows were drawn together as he slowly shook Meg's hand. "Meghan Bailey."

"That's right, sir."

His dad narrowed his eyes and cut a glance toward Jax.

Was his dad upset? Annoyed that he didn't know every little thing about Jax's life?

"How many weeks have you been seeing each other?" His dad released Meg's hand and folded his arms.

Okay, with introductions over, Jax was ready to ditch his parents.

"You should come to our—" his mom started to say, but his dad cut her off.

"How many weeks?" his dad repeated.

Jax frowned. What was up with his dad?

"About three weeks," Meg said.

His dad's gaze shifted to Meg. "Since the day of his *accident?*" he said in a low voice.

What the hell? "Dad," Jax said in a warning voice. Apparently his dad had read the police report and recognized her name.

His dad held up his hand, his gaze still on Meg. "You're Meghan Bailey, the woman who nearly killed my son?"

His mom gasped. "No."

"Listen, both of you," Jax said, moving between his dad and Meg. "Meg is the woman who slammed on her brakes when I stepped in front of her car because I was fuming after learning about how much you've been donating to the Flyers."

Thankfully, no one was close enough to overhear the Emerson family dispute, but Jax didn't care if they were. He was sick of his dad's control and manipulation.

His dad's mouth opened, then shut. "You're out of line, son."

Jax took a step closer and lowered his voice. "No. *You're* out of line. And whatever is going through your mind right now, just stop thinking it. Now."

His dad blinked. "I need to speak with you as soon as possible. *Privately.*"

The man was unbelievable.

"Todd," his mom said. "I'm sure Meghan is a lovely woman, and she didn't mean Jax any harm."

His dad didn't blink, and neither did Jax.

From behind Jax, Meg said, "I've got to say goodbye to Nashelle, so I'll, um, talk to you later."

Jax didn't turn, keeping his gaze on his dad. "Meghan, can you meet me by the locker room?"

"Okay." Her voice sounded faint, but truthfully, he was glad that she was leaving the circus that was his parents.

He watched her climb up the stairs again, then he turned back to his dad. "Spill it. Now. You have thirty seconds."

"Privately, I said."

Jax folded his arms. "Now."

His dad glanced about, then set his hands on his hips. "I've filed a lawsuit against Meghan Bailey. She'll be getting papers served tomorrow. I've done extensive research on her as a person and her business. She's not someone any son of mine should be involved with."

Jax felt like he was watching a bad horror flick where the reality was so skewed, it wasn't even close to reality. "Please tell me you're joking." He looked at his mom, but her eyes were wide with disbelief.

"I'm not joking," his dad said. "She set you up. She's after your money."

If there was ever a time Jax had wanted to break his dad's nose, this was it.

"Cancel the lawsuit," Jax ground out. "And if you don't, you'll be hearing from my attorney." He turned then and headed away from the man he couldn't stand to look in the eyes any longer.

He felt like throwing up. How could his dad do this? If anything, Meg should be suing *Jax* for stepping in front of her

174

car and causing damage. He slammed into the locker room, and everyone looked over at him. No one said a word. There had obviously been some celebrating going on, but now the locker room went dead silent.

Jax changed and showered and dressed without speaking to anyone. He needed to tell Meg about the lawsuit, even if it was stopped before any papers were served to her. But how was he going to tell her what his dad had done? Would she hate Jax too?

TWENTY

JAX STILL HADN'T come out of the locker room, and Meg was starting to get antsy. Every player had come out, and she'd felt more and more conspicuous as they noticed her. A couple of them said hi—like Lucas. Nate merely lifted his brows as he passed. No words were exchanged.

Maybe Jax had gone another way? Maybe he was still talking to his dad?

Whatever it was, Meg knew that it couldn't be good. Her stomach was in knots since meeting his parents. Only seeing Jax and knowing he was good and that they were still dating would ease her heavy heart.

Yeah, she had known his parents would find out at some point that she was the one involved in the accident. But the fact that his dad knew her name was kind of odd. But he seemed to be an observant guy, so maybe that was why? She honestly didn't know.

Another player exited the locker room. No, it was the head coach. Lindon. He glanced at Meg as he passed, gave a nod, then continued on his way.

So even the coach had left. Where was Jax?

She checked her cell. It had been a full forty minutes, and still no Jax. Maybe she should just go home.

Nashelle was likely at her place by now, and it wasn't like Meg could call her grandma to come pick her up. No matter; she opened the Lyft app on her phone. The prices were at a premium right now because of the hockey game. She selected her location and was about to book a ride when footsteps sounded. She looked up to see Jax come out of the locker room.

He was dressed up more than usual, wearing a navy blazer over a white button-down shirt open at the collar. His jeans looked expensive, and his shoes were polished dark-brown loafers.

Meg straightened from where she'd been leaning against the wall. She suddenly felt underdressed, wearing the hockey jersey she'd bought on a whim right before the game. Jax's gray eyes scanned her, then met her eyes. She couldn't read his expression. He'd just won a huge game, then got into an argument with his dad over her, and now . . . he was dressed up for what?

"Sorry to keep you waiting," he said, stopping in front of her. In one hand, he carried a large duffle. "I had to make some calls."

She nodded, because her throat felt too tight to speak. Phone calls having to do with what? Not that it was any of her business, but obviously he didn't want her overhearing.

"What's that on your phone?" he asked.

She looked down at the app she'd opened. "Oh, I wasn't sure how long you'd be, so I was going to order a Lyft." She looked up at him, trying to read him, trying to figure out what she should be saying or doing.

"Cancel it."

"I haven't scheduled it yet," she said, slipping her phone

into her purse. He was still staring at her, rather intently. "Is . . . everything okay?"

"There're some things we need to talk about," he said.

Meg's stomach plummeted. So things with his dad had gone awry, over *her,* and now Jax was going to let her down easy. Her eyes stung, and her throat felt raw. But she wouldn't cry, not with Jax watching her.

"Okay," she said in as light a tone as possible, but it came out as more of a squeak.

"But first we need to go meet my agent."

" *We?* "

"Yeah, I'd like you to come, if that's all right?"

Meg's mind whirled. What did all this mean? Was he going to break things off with her or not? Why would he want her in a meeting with his agent? And . . . he was waiting for her to answer. "Um, okay. Although I feel really underdressed now."

The edge of his mouth lifted as his gaze dipped, then met her eyes again. "You look fine. I like you wearing my number."

She let out a breath. This was good, right? The butterflies in her stomach thought so.

"Come on," he said, reaching for her hand.

Her heart leapt at the touch of his skin against hers and at how his fingers linked into an easy grasp. She was still dying to know what he wanted to talk about, but for now, she was happy with his affection. Because she was pretty sure he wouldn't hold her hand if he planned on breaking things off.

He was quiet as they walked out of the arena to the parking lot, and Meg was okay with that. The tension in her stomach had eased, and Jax was holding her hand.

"Where are we going?" she asked as they neared his truck.

"Clint's hotel," Jax said. "He and Marcus are meeting us in the hotel restaurant."

Meg turned to face him as he unlocked the passenger door for her. "I really don't want to be in the way. I mean, I'm sort of the odd woman out."

"You're with me," Jax said. "There's nothing more to discuss."

"Oh, really?"

"Really." He set his duffle bag in the back seat, then moved closer to her, his gaze intent on her. "What are you worried about, Meghan?"

She looked away from his intense gaze. "I'm being paranoid, I guess. I mean, you introduced me to your parents, and look how that turned out. Meeting your agent feels really personal."

Jax's jaw clenched, and he put a hand on the truck next to her, bringing their bodies in closer proximity. "We'll talk about my parents later. But for now, I don't want you to think twice about them. Trust me on this, okay?"

She nodded.

"Good." He lifted his hand and brushed his fingers along her neck. "When I saw you show up in my jersey tonight, I was a happy man." His fingers traced the collar of the jersey, then rested on her shoulder.

"You're easy to please, then," she whispered, placing a hand on his chest.

His gaze remained intense. "I think it's just you."

Meg rose up on her toes and curled her fingers around the lapels of his blazer. His gaze darkened just before she pressed her mouth against his. Jax groaned and pulled her close, deepening the kiss. Meg's heart pounded both with relief and the slow intensity of Jax's kissing.

This man had somehow worked his way into her heart and psyche. A passing car's headlights flashing against them made Meg aware of how very public this kiss was.

She drew away, even though Jax didn't relinquish his hold.

"Keep kissing me like that, and you're not going home tonight."

Meg's entire body flushed hot. "I just missed you, I guess."

His brow lifted. "When?"

Had she confessed too much? "Whenever I'm not with you." There, if that wasn't plain speaking, she didn't know what was.

Jax leaned down and kissed her ever so lightly. "I miss you too."

She smiled, her heart soaring.

Another car passed, and Jax said, "We should go, even though the last thing I want is to be around other people right now."

The drive to the hotel wasn't far, and Jax left the truck in the hands of the valet. Then he led Meg inside. Her nerves buzzed in anticipation. She'd never felt more like part of a couple than she did now with Jax, and a sense of surrealness filled her.

Heads turned as they walked through the lobby. Jax would make an impressive figure even if he weren't beloved by all of Chicago. And he was with her, holding her hand, telling her things like he missed her and he wanted her to be part of his meeting with his agent.

Three men sat at a table near the window of the restaurant. When they all three stood, Meg had no trouble picking out Clint, and next to him stood a guy with a thick beard who looked like he could be Clint's brother.

The third man must be Marcus, the agent. He was shorter, with brown hair, fashionably spikey. He wore a nice suit, though no tie.

"Jax Emerson," Marcus said. "Nice to meet you at last."

The two men clasped hands.

"Thanks for waiting," Jax said. "This is Meghan Bailey."

"Hello," Marcus said, extending his hand. "Nice to meet you, Meghan."

She smiled, hoping that she didn't look as nervous as she felt.

"And this is Clint," Jax continued the introductions, "and his brother, Grizz."

The bearded guy grinned. "That's me."

Clearly that was a nickname, right? She remembered Jax telling her that Clint's brother was a pro baseball player, repped by Marcus as well. The two brothers gave Jax a bro hug and shook hands with Meg. Wow. She was way out of her element here. Every person in the restaurant was taking surreptitious glances at their group. Meg didn't blame them. She could hardly believe she was with this group of guys herself.

They all sat down again, and Jax indicated for her to sit by Marcus, which put her between Jax and Marcus. Making her more a part of the conversation and not on the fringes of it like she expected. She had nothing to contribute, after all.

Jax draped his arm across the back of her chair, not touching her but making it clear that they were together.

Clint just smiled at the two of them, and Grizz sat back, browsing the menu.

"You guys didn't have to wait to order," Jax said.

"We weren't waiting for you," Clint said. "Grizz here is taking forever to decide."

Grizz chuckled. "I'm almost there. Three more minutes tops."

Clint shook his head with a laugh.

"Perfect. That's all the time we'll need too," Jax said,

sliding a menu between him and Meg and opening it. "What sounds good?" he said more quietly, just to Meg.

She seriously doubted she'd be able to eat a thing surrounded by these guys. But everyone seemed focused on her now. Okay . . . She scanned the salads and pastas and steak and seafood options. "Um, the Chinese chicken salad looks good."

"That's what I thought," Grizz said. "I'm getting that too."

Was he joking? Meg was going to be a blushing mess.

"With a top sirloin on the side," Grizz added.

Jax chuckled. "Thought so. I'm going to get the top sirloin too."

It seemed the waiter had keen hearing, because he suddenly appeared at the table. "Ready, folks?"

Everyone put in their orders, and Meg slowly started to relax. They were all normal men when all was said and done, right? And she knew Jax, so that should make her feel comfortable.

"So we've all been doing some brainstorming while waiting for you to get here," Marcus began.

"Should I be worried?" Jax rumbled.

The guys laughed, and Meg smiled.

"Your stats are through the roof," Marcus continued. "You're gonna have your pick once we announce you're up for trade."

"Are there issues with my contract? Did you already look into that?"

"I did. Scott sent everything over, and I was able to review your contract before tonight's game. The opt-out clauses started two years ago." Marcus picked up his water glass and took a sip. "We'll have to go through protocol stuff, but I'll take care of all that."

Jax nodded. His fingers brushed against Meg's shoulder absently.

Marcus took another drink of his water. Meg wondered if the man was nervous. He seemed pretty calm and collected, but he was drinking a lot of water.

"There's another option," Marcus said, his tone sounding unsure.

"What's that?"

Marcus glanced at Clint and Grizz before answering. "It was suggested by Clint, actually."

Jax's fingers stopped moving on Meg's shoulder. "Spill it."

"Well," Marcus said, resting his elbows on the table and leaning forward, "we can renegotiate your Flyers contract."

The tenseness coming from Jax was palpable. "That's not at all why I hired you, Marcus—"

"Think about it, Jax," Clint cut in. "The negotiation can stipulate that your paycheck is not predicated on donations or sponsors."

Jax didn't say anything for a moment. "Can that be mandated?"

"We can write anything into the contract we want, and if they sign off on it, then it's a done deal." Marcus tapped the table. "Think of it this way. You're the face of the Chicago Flyers right now. The last two games have been sold out completely. This hasn't happened for years. Hockey is resurging throughout the city. That kids' hockey camp you guys did? Brilliant."

Jax nodded, but his tone didn't sound convinced. "You know how personal my reasons are. I've put in plenty of time to the Flyers, eight years to be exact."

"Career's just getting started," Grizz deadpanned.

Jax scoffed but made no retort.

Marcus reached into a computer bag set by his chair. He pulled out a file, then opened it. "Here are the fundraising numbers from the youth hockey camp." Turning the sheet so that Jax could read it, Meg caught a glimpse of the final number.

"Wow," Jax said. "Over a million for a one-day event?"

"This is everything, from the camp to the spectator fees, to the silent auction going on in the lobby, and finally, direct donations that came in."

Jax didn't speak for a moment, and Clint jumped in. "That's a real boost to the Northbrook club. Where are you going with this, Marcus?"

"Well." Marcus leaned back in his chair. "I'll tell you where this is going. The manager, Mr. White, took my call earlier today. Said that they're starting weekend training clinics. They've got over two hundred kids registered already, from ages twelve and up. They're even considering putting together a few girl-specific clinics. Come the next club season, they'll have enough teams and competition with neighboring cities and states to make girls' hockey viable in Chicago."

Jax picked up the fundraising report. "These numbers are separate from the fundraiser gala that Bree Stone spearheaded last month, right?"

"Right," Marcus confirmed. "The youth hockey camp fundraiser goes exclusively toward the kids themselves. Scholarships, equipment, training, hiring coaching staff ... the whole works. With you and other former Northbrook athletes putting your face to this, the money will continue coming in."

"How do we continue putting our face to this?" Jax asked.

"More hockey camps, more fundraisers. We can get creative, especially in the off-season. Bree Stone sent me over a list of suggestions." Marcus filed the papers away as two waiters approached, carrying trays loaded with food.

"I can still help with the hockey camp living somewhere

else," Jax said. "All my other former teammates are doing that."

"Right," Marcus said. "But having one of the players in Chicago would make a difference."

"Here you are, sir." The waiter broke into the conversation and set down two plates in front of Grizz.

Meg hid a smile. He really had ordered two full meals.

No one at the table seemed surprised, though. When everyone was served and drinks were refilled, Meg picked up her fork. She had yet to say one word in this meeting of sorts, but Jax's constant presence next to her still made her feel included.

The group ate for a few minutes in silence, and it was Jax who finally spoke first. "Rocco had another idea for the Northbrook club. I talked to him just before coming here tonight."

Meg couldn't explain the relief that coursed through her. His phone call in the locker room had been with Rocco. Why she was happy about that, she wasn't sure.

Jax had everyone's full attention at the table. "It's a bit wild, but you know Rocco."

The three other guys nodded. "So, Rocco thinks I should mandate to my dad to donate his generous hockey funds to Northbrook instead of to the Flyers. Then see if the Flyers will extend my contract on their own."

Marcus set down his fork and narrowed his eyes. "That's not a bad idea."

Jax reached for his drink, and after a swallow, he said, "Yeah, except another complication has arisen with my dad, so cutting ties with him might be the best thing for everyone involved."

Meg didn't know what Jax was talking about, but his tone was filled with frustration.

Marcus was unconcerned. "Well, tonight is about making introductions and throwing out a few options. We'll know real information when I contact the other teams about your contract options and availability for trade."

Jax nodded. "Fair enough."

Meg could practically feel the weight on his shoulders, and her curiosity only mounted. What was going on with his dad now? Is that what he wanted to talk to her about later? Whatever it was, it seemed he wasn't about to discuss it over dinner.

For the next thirty minutes, Clint and Jax traded team stories, then Clint talked about his service in the military.

"Meg's brother's in the military," Jax said.

Clint turned his gaze on Meg. "Oh, really? Which division?"

"Army," she said. "He's stationed in the Middle East right now."

Clint asked more questions, and she answered the ones that she knew. It wasn't like her brother could tell her much, and their relationship was relegated to the occasional email.

When the meal was over, Jax rose from the table. He shook hands with Marcus, promising to talk again over the next few days.

"Stellar game, by the way," Marcus said.

"Thanks, man."

Grizz clapped Jax on the shoulder. "Good luck with everything."

"Thanks," Jax said.

"And tell your brother thanks for his service," Grizz told Meg.

"I will," she said, her voice probably breathless. Standing next to these guys, she felt so tiny.

"Talk to you soon," Clint told Jax. Then to Meg, he said, "Keep him out of trouble."

She laughed. "I plan to."

After all the goodbyes, Jax walked with Meg outside of the hotel, holding her hand again. He seemed to be lost in thought as they waited for the valet to bring the truck. When Jax opened the door to the truck for her to climb in, he said, "Can we go somewhere to talk?"

Here it was . . . "We're pretty close to my grandma's. She'll be asleep, so we won't have to worry about being interrupted."

Jax nodded. "Okay."

How serious was this, and how long was it going to take? Meg watched him walk around the truck, her mind churning with questions and her heart thumping with anticipation.

TWENTY-ONE

THERE WAS REALLY no easy way to tell Meg that his father had filed a lawsuit against her, except for just telling her straight out.

With a heavy heart, Jax walked with her into her grandma's house. The place was quaint and smelled of pine and cinnamon. A Christmas tree glittered in the corner of the front room, but Meg led him into the kitchen and turned on the lights.

The place was cozy and very, very blue. Blue walls, blue countertops, frilly blue curtains, and blue placemats on the table. "Is blue your favorite color, or your grandma's?"

Meg smiled. "Oh, this is all my grandma's doing."

Meg might be smiling, but he could also see that she was a bit hesitant, and probably curious as to what he'd kept hinting at.

"Do you want a drink or anything? There might still be cookies left from when I made them the other day."

"You make cookies too?"

"They're just chocolate chip."

Jax blinked. "I'm fine for now, but I might take a rain check for later."

"Okay." She opened a cupboard, and Jax watched her pull down a couple of glasses, then fill them with ice and water.

When she turned, he was still watching her. He really, really liked her wearing the hockey jersey with his number. And her jeans were pretty cute too. He also liked her hair pulled back, off her neck. She had an elegant neck, and he was well familiar with the smoothness of her skin. He really didn't want to have this conversation. He'd rather pull her into his arms and show her how beautiful he found her.

Meg crossed to the table and set down the two water glasses. "Sit down, Jax. You're making me nervous."

"Fair enough." He pulled out a chair and sat. Everything suddenly felt formal, and he reached for the ice water.

Meg drank some from her glass too, then folded her hands atop the table.

"My dad gave me some bad news tonight," he said, diving right in. "You may or may not know this about him, but he's the kind of guy who sues to get his way in most of his business deals. He always has a long list of justifications, of course. Some of them make sense, but in reality, it's how he gets his way."

Meg watched him with those deep-green eyes of hers, and he was pretty sure he'd already confused her.

"When my dad found out your name, he recognized it from the police report."

Meg nodded. "I thought that might be the case."

Jax exhaled. "You see, he got ahold of it—even though he shouldn't have been allowed access. He found out the driver's name—you—and he did some investigating into your background."

Her brows pinched together. "Like a background check to see if I was a criminal or something?"

"That was only part of it," Jax said. "He knows what I

wrote in my own incident report that I filled out at the hospital, which, of course, confirmed your innocence. Still, my dad wanted to know if you were impaired or had restrictions on your driver's license."

Meg's face flushed. "There's nothing for him to find."

"Doesn't matter. My dad's like a pit bull," Jax said. "He can't be called off a scent until he finds what he wants." He hated the wariness that had settled in Meg's gaze. He hadn't even gotten to the hard part.

"What did he find?"

"He looked into your financials." Jax rubbed the back of his neck. "My dad wanted to know what he could sue you for." He knew that the news would be hard to deliver, but he never expected Meg to lose all color.

Her gaze shifted from his.

He reached for her hand. "My dad's going to drop the lawsuit. I told him that we're dating, and I explained the real reason I walked into the middle of the street without looking."

Meg tugged her hand away and folded her arms. She was staring at the tabletop.

Jax had never seen Meg mad before, but he was pretty sure this was it. "I told him it wasn't your fault, and besides, he can't sue on behalf of me."

"What did he say?" she said in a quiet voice, still not looking at him.

"My dad thinks that basic logic doesn't apply to him, so the fact that I'm the one who was hit and not him, and that I'm a grown adult, doesn't faze him."

Meg didn't say anything for a moment. Then she wiped at her eyes. "Well, I did hit you with my car. There's no denying that."

"Hey." Jax was on his feet in an instant. He moved around the table and drew her to her feet. "Don't even think that way. We both know it was *me*. We've been over this, okay?"

She nodded but wouldn't meet his eyes.

"Meghan, please, stay with me," Jax said. "There's more."

Slowly, she lifted her gaze. "What?" she whispered.

"My dad accused you of trying to use me, you know, like some women might use a guy who has a lot of money. Like you hit me on purpose, and now you're dating me so that I'll help you financially."

Her eyes rounded. "That's ridiculous. I didn't even know you—"

Jax set his hands on her shoulders. "I know. My dad made some gross assumptions that aren't true. But I needed to come completely clean with you so that we can talk about some other things."

She stepped away from him, and he dropped his hands. "I don't know if I can handle anything more," she said. "I sort of hate your dad right now."

Jax nodded. "Believe me, I get that. Because I've been there myself. Many times."

Meg moved past Jax to the kitchen sink. She turned around and leaned against it, folding her arms again. "Well, whatever it is, I guess your dad didn't turn you against me. I mean, you took me to dinner with your agent and everything."

Her voice trembled, and Jax didn't want her crying again. He moved closer, but not so close that she'd feel crowded.

"My dad sent over some texts after our argument," Jax said. "Apparently he found out that you're about to lose your store."

The surprise in Meg's eyes was plain, but then the flush on her face told him that his dad had the right information. It didn't matter to Jax, though, whether Meg had a million dollars or was in heavy debt. Money was money, and it should never control a relationship. He'd learned that the hard way from his dad.

"Is it true?" he asked in a quiet tone.

When Meg nodded, Jax felt literal pain in his chest. He knew how much she loved her store and her career.

"What are you going to do?" he continued.

She visibly swallowed, gripping the sides of the counter she was leaning against. "I'm going to liquidate in January. Today I gave my employees a heads-up so they can start looking elsewhere." She wiped at a fallen tear. "My part-timers are quitting now with a small severance. Nashelle is looking but will probably stay until the bitter end. My, uh, lease has gone up over the past few months, and with the combination of decreased business and not getting full rent for my apartment, I just keep going into more and more debt each month."

"Why aren't you getting full rent?"

"I'm renting to a friend of mine," Meg said. "She's a single mom with two little kids. She can't afford the full price."

"But you're losing your livelihood over it? That's a huge sacrifice."

"No, it's the higher lease on the boutique and the stagnant sales," Meg said. "I could always get a new renter or sell the place at a loss. I just can't move back there, not after Blaine helped me pick it out. And I'll be fine. I'm going to build up my website and shift to online exclusive." She shrugged as if it were no big deal, but she wasn't fooling him. "It's the wave of the future, right? Online sales."

Jax took a step closer. "I could help you."

Meg blinked. "What are you talking about?"

"You know," he hedged. "I could pay your shop lease for a few months."

Her brows shot up. "You can't pay my lease. It's . . . it's a business, and sometimes they fail—"

"Meghan." Jax reached her and braced his hands on either side of her. "Let me help you. This is your dream. And there are only so many wells I can build in Africa."

The edges of her mouth lifted, but she shook her head. "No, I couldn't let you do that. It's too much. Way too much. I don't want to take advantage of you."

Jax rubbed a thumb over her hand. "It's not taking advantage when I'm offering."

Her gaze held his, and he saw the shift in her eyes as she considered his offer.

"You're sweet, Jax . . ."

"So I've been told."

Her smile was fleeting. "I've been dealing with this since long before I met you, and well, I've already looked into all my options. Getting an investor, applying for another loan, selling the apartment, all of it . . . the best financial sense is to move everything to the online store."

"Meghan," he said in a soft voice. "I can help. This isn't an impulse offer. The moment I thought of it, I had no doubt it was the right thing to do."

"It's tempting, believe me," she said, resting a hand on his forearm. "But even though I like you, a lot, and you're really sweet to offer such a huge thing, the reality is that I've done this on my own. From the ground up. And I need to do the rest on my own."

"It's okay to get help sometimes."

"I know," she said, lifting her chin. "But to accept help now . . . it's like another defeat on top of what I'm already losing."

Jax stared into her green eyes. "Is it me? I mean, if someone else offered, another investor, would you turn them down?"

Her gaze shifted then. "How would it look if I accepted your offer after what your dad accused me of?"

Jax hung his head and released a sigh. "Sometimes I hate my dad too."

She moved her hand up farther on his arm. "Look, you have enough to deal with. Your parents, your contract, your career. Don't worry about me. You really don't need more burdens."

Jax lifted his head. "You're not a burden, Meghan." He moved one hand to her hip and drew her close. Then he leaned down and whispered in her ear. "I want to help you. It would make me happy."

She slid her arms around his neck, and this gave him hope. "You're sweet, Jax, but my answer's still no."

"I can be very convincing," he said, kissing her neck.

Her hold tightened about him. "I can be very stubborn."

He chuckled. "Think about it, okay?"

She arched back so that she met his gaze. He saw only resolution there.

"My mind's made up, so you can either drop it and kiss me or you can say good night."

The choice wasn't hard. He decided to drop it for now and, yeah, kiss her. Thoroughly.

An hour later, when he walked into his house, he called Rocco to give him an update. He'd been ignoring the guy's texts long enough. When Jax had called him in the locker room, he had been desperate for an outsider's advice. His dad had gotten into his head before, and he'd needed to think straight. The accusations his dad had made about Meg were ridiculous, but there was always that small seed of doubt inside of Jax that women only saw him for his money. While he didn't want to believe that of Meg, Rocco had been a good sounding board.

Rocco had agreed with Jax one hundred percent. Meg was innocent of the accusations, but Rocco had also suggested that Jax test her by offering to pay her lease. Jax didn't like the sound of that, but throughout the evening, he'd decided he wanted to offer anyway. Not as a test but as a sincere offer. Because he did want to help her. He already knew his feelings for her were growing stronger by the day—by the hour, it seemed—and there was no reason he *shouldn't* help her.

"So?" Rocco said, answering the phone on the first ring. "What did she say when you offered to invest?"

"She turned me down," Jax said, scratching Sheriff's head, which was currently resting on his knee as he sat on the living room couch. "And I was pretty persuasive."

Rocco scoffed. "Don't need those kinds of details, man. But it sounds like you have your answer."

"Yeah, but I do want to invest," Jax said. "I wasn't testing her. I think it would be a win-win."

"How so?" His tone was definitely skeptical.

"Well . . . I want to help her. This is her dream, and she's gone after it. Not many people can say that." He told Rocco about how she was losing money renting her apartment to a single mom and how she had several employees dependent on her.

"Huh."

"That's all you have to say?" Jax said.

"I have a lot to say, but I'm not sure you're ready to hear it."

Jax leaned back on the couch and sighed. Sheriff didn't like the change in position, because it meant no more head scratching. "I don't think I want to hear it."

"Yeah, well, all I'm gonna say is that you're in deep, my friend," Rocco said. "I just hope that you aren't jumping in too fast. You guys haven't known each other long."

"I know." Jax closed his eyes. "She's different, though. I'm afraid that I'm more invested than her. Maybe it's a rebound thing."

"You told me Lacy was over a year ago."

"She was."

"This isn't a rebound thing, then," Rocco said, then he went silent for a moment.

Was Jax falling for Meghan? Already? Was that possible after only a few weeks?

"You could still help her, though," Rocco said in a thoughtful tone.

"How?"

"Find out who owns the building," Rocco said. "Property owners are public record. Find out how deep she's in this. Maybe the landlord will give her a grace period."

Jax kind of liked the idea, but whether he found out she was about to go under this month or in three months, it wouldn't matter. He still wanted to help her. "What if I contact her landlord and make a couple of payments?"

Rocco blew out a breath. "Without telling her."

Jax rose from the couch and walked down the hall to his office. "Ask for forgiveness later?"

Rocco scoffed. "I don't know, man. That's a big move. It might upset her."

"I'd be helping her, though. Saving her store. Something she loves, right?" Jax opened up the laptop on the desk.

"Right . . ." Rocco's tone was hesitant.

"All right, I'm going to do some research."

"Okay, but you better think through this," Rocco said. "You don't want to step where you're not wanted."

"Got it." Jax hung up with the guy and pulled up the browser. Then he started the search for property owners.

TWENTY-TWO

MEG UNLOCKED THE front door to her boutique. It was surreal to think that in about a month, she'd have vacated the place. Jax was right, she did love her boutique. She'd been running it for five years now, and it was her home away from home. Well, really her home, because since the fiasco with Blaine, she'd left her beloved one-bedroom apartment, bought the new place, been dumped by Blaine, and then moved in with her grandma. Nothing like going backward in life.

But it would be fine. Just like she had told Jax. Online shopping was a huge presence in the clothing market anyway. She might have to shift from high-end fashion to more midgrade stuff. She'd swallow that bitter pill later. The best thing she could do right now was get as much as she could out of the current stock.

She had about half an hour before Nashelle would show up for her shift, and Meg took her time going through the rounders, straightening clothing and adjusting some of the racks. Every couple of days she'd redress the mannequins in the front window, and she decided to put out the New Year's Eve dresses.

Yeah, Christmas shopping was still going on, but it was never too early to shop for New Year's, right?

She decided on a red dress and a silver dress. Once the mannequins were dressed, she went to the register, where she'd left the discount list. Twenty percent off all scarves and blouses. She hoped this would bring in more customers. Maybe even some new ones. Last night, she'd scheduled an email and Facebook post to go out to all their subscribers. And this morning, a sign she'd ordered would be delivered.

She cringed at the thought of a garish sale sign in the front window, but it couldn't be helped. Every step would be hard, and she'd make it through. Somehow.

Jax's offer was generous, sweet, and oh so tempting. But she couldn't be in debt to him, or any man, again. She'd invested enough into her relationship with Blaine. She didn't want things to be like that with Jax, didn't want his dad's predictions to come true. Dating Jax was something she had to pinch herself over, but she'd never take advantage of him.

Her independent heart was just too stubborn.

The front door's chimes sounded, and Nashelle walked in.

"Hey, there. You're early," Meg said, offering a smile she didn't feel.

"Yeah, well, the dog was up half the night again crying," Nashelle said.

Her normally dark-smudged eye makeup didn't need any embellishment. The circles were violet beneath her eyes.

"You should have called me," Meg said. "Taken the morning off."

Nashelle set her leather bag onto the counter. "No, the vet bills are going to kill me. I need the paycheck."

The comment felt like a knife to the heart, although Meg knew Nashelle didn't mean it that way. Here Meg was letting all of her employees go, but she'd also come up with an option that might at least help Nashelle.

"So, I was thinking that if you don't find something full-time soon, you could help me out part-time for a bit."

Nashelle's dark eyes flashed to Meg's. "Helping you with the transition?"

"Yeah." Meg released a breath. "I can't promise much, but at least something to tide you over. If you need it."

"I need it." Nashelle dug in her bag. "Even if I find something full-time, I'll need any extra hours. Here it is." She pulled out her phone. "I wanted to show you an Instagram shopping account. I think you need to start selling directly from Instagram."

For the next while, Meg browsed Instagram pages to see how they'd set up their selling process. This was all way out of her element. Nashelle set up the sales signs around the store, and their first customer came in around eleven, two hours after the store had opened. Frustrating. At least she bought two items.

By the afternoon, things had picked up, but Meg was still dwelling more and more on Jax's offer. She knew if she confided in Nashelle, the woman would urge her to take it. Which was why Meg had to keep it to herself.

She planned to go settle the final payment before the bank closed today. She usually did everything online, but she'd be closing out the account, and she needed to give them a heads-up so that she didn't get automatically billed in another thirty days. After that was done, she'd be giving her landlord notice as well. In their contract, he'd asked for thirty days, and she planned to honor that.

The day passed slowly, and the only bright spots were Jax's occasional texts. His team would be flying to Denver tonight for tomorrow's game against Jax's former teammate, Declan Rivera.

By four, his texts had died off, and she guessed he was at the airport. He'd only be gone a couple of days, and she already missed him. Not that she'd tell him that. He might renew the conversation about being her investor. She had to stay strong in her determination. Still, everything seemed gloomy with the darkening day.

Fitting that the wind picked up, blowing in a snowstorm. No one would be coming in now. She wished she could close down early, but she hated to close before the posted hours.

"You can leave before the storm gets too bad," Meg told Nashelle.

"Are you sure?" Nashelle said. "You gonna be okay?"

"Yeah, sure." Meg put on a smile. Nashelle had asked her more than once today if she was okay. Besides the store closing, she was fine. Just had to get over this hurdle.

After Nashelle left, Meg went back to Instagram and took notes on things she liked and ideas that might cross over to her plans. Then she added news of the sale on the Insta page. They only had about a hundred followers, but maybe that would grow with a stronger online presence.

Her mind wandered to Jax and what he was doing. Probably sitting on a plane. Hopefully they got out before the storm. At six sharp, she turned off the lights and exited out the back way. The wind had blown the snow into a frenzy, and she held up her arm to shield her eyes from the pelting snow. She made it to her car, but the windows were caked in icy snow, so she started the car, then used her ice scraper to get the windows decent.

The streets were a mess, and she was grateful her bank stayed open until seven, because it took her almost forty-five minutes to make the usually ten-minute drive. After hurrying inside the bank, she took a minute to thaw out from the bitter wind outside.

It was another ten minutes before she was seated across from an account manager. She gave out her information and explained that she wanted to close out the auto-pay.

"You'll have to pay December's payment right now, then," the woman, whose nametag read *Lisa*, said.

"Sure thing," Meg said. "I can do a transfer from my savings into the payment account."

"Very well." Lisa typed on the keyboard, then frowned.

At her silence, Meg said, "What is it? I should have enough in savings."

"It's not that," Lisa says. "I don't see a balance on the payment account."

"It's under my business name, Meg's Loft."

"Yeah, I have that pulled up." Lisa rotated the monitor. "The balance due was paid this morning."

Meg was confused. "It already transferred? It's supposed to come out next week."

Lisa tapped on the keyboard. "Hang on." She studied the screen. "The payment came from another account . . . from another bank, in fact."

This was bizarre. Maybe the landlord had made the payment and wanted her to pay him directly now? That was what he'd proposed years ago, but Meg had felt safer about doing everything through a banking institution, so they'd set up the payment system.

"Can you tell me who it was?" She fully expected Lisa to say Darrel Smith, but she didn't.

"Oh." Lisa's brows pulled together. "It came from a personal account. Jackson Emerson."

Meg didn't move, couldn't think. "Are you sure?" she breathed.

"Uh, yes," Lisa continued. "Says here it transferred around ten this morning. And there's an automatic payment set up as well. No cutoff date."

Meg swallowed. "So the same amount will be paid next month?"

"Correct." Lisa tapped a few more things. "Do you still want to close the account?"

"Yes, but I need to make a phone call first." She looked down at her cell phone. Jax was probably still in the air. She looked back at Lisa's curious gaze. "I'll, uh, be back in the morning and get things straightened out."

Meg hurried out of the bank, her mind reeling. She didn't even register the worsened storm until she felt like her breath had been stolen by the wind. She climbed into her car and just sat for a moment. Numbness pulsed through her. What had Jax done? She didn't know whether to cry or be angry.

She'd told him no ... and yet ... did he think she wouldn't find out? Wouldn't know that her lease was suddenly paid in full? Meg smacked the steering wheel. She didn't want a man who didn't respect her wishes. Her feelings.

Jax wasn't like Blaine, no, but this was still similar to the line of thought when someone thought they knew what was best for her. When someone else believed he was in charge of her life.

Meg exhaled a shaky breath. She could go home and cry, and then when Jax's plane landed, she'd call him. Tell him to stay out of her boutique business. He'd hurt her, maybe unintentionally, but the worst thing about it was that this was something his dad might do.

The interior of the car was nearly freezing, and Meg pushed on the ignition starter, but nothing happened. The maintenance light blinked on. "No!" she cried. "Don't do this now!"

The battery was brand new. She hadn't left lights on. The car had been running fine twenty minutes ago. She tried again. Then again. She pounded the steering wheel, this time for a different reason.

She zipped up her coat, then she called roadside assistance. No one answered at first, which was weird, so she called back. The operator that came on sounded frazzled.

"Can I help you?"

"My car won't start," Meg said. "I just had the battery replaced, though, so I don't know what's going on."

"All right, ma'am, what's your location?"

Meg gave it to her.

"It looks like there are significant delays in your area because of a storm," the woman said. "Estimated arrival of a work truck is two and a half to three hours."

Meg's breath stalled. "That long? Aren't there any back-ups for storms?"

"Those are the backups," the woman said.

"Okay," Meg said. "Book me, but if I find another option I'll cancel." She couldn't sit in the car for three hours, and the bank had already closed. She craned her neck to see that yep, she was in the financial district, and nothing looked open around her.

"Very well, ma'am," the dispatcher said. "You'll get an update call a bit later with a more firm time."

After she hung up, she considered her options of whom to call. Nashelle? No, her car was a beater. Grandma? Not in this weather. Her other employees used public transportation. Her phone rang, and Meg wondered if luck was on her side and the dispatcher was calling back.

To her surprise, Jax's name flashed across the screen. How long had his flight been? And did she want to talk to him *now*? Her thoughts were scattered as it was, and she needed to get someplace warm.

"Hello?" she said, her heart thudding.

"Hey." His tone was warm, easy.

This annoyed her. He didn't know she knew about the lease payment, or maybe he had the arrogance to not think it a big deal to go behind her back.

"Are you in Wyoming already?" she said, hoping her voice was steady and not hinting at the anger bubbling in her chest.

"Nah. Our flight was cancelled. We'll fly out early tomorrow, or as soon as the runways are cleared."

He was still in Chicago.

She closed her eyes. She needed to confront him—now, before it gnawed a hole in her gut. But she was also seeing her breath inside the car as the icy weather crept in.

"Are you stuck at the airport?" she asked.

"I just got home," he said. "A truck comes in handy in these situations. What about you? Did you get to your grandma's okay?"

"Not exactly."

She hated the concern she heard in his voice when he said, "What's going on? Are you stuck at your boutique?"

"I made it to the bank, but now my car won't start," she said. "Roadside assistance is delayed for a few hours, but I think Nashelle can pick me up." *Lie.*

"I'll come," Jax said. Easy. Natural. Like they were dating and it was no big deal. Bailing her out with car troubles *and* financial troubles.

"I'm fine, I don't want to tell Nashelle to turn around." Was she really going to follow through with this lie? Her body had started to shiver.

"What's she driving?"

"A . . . Hyundai Elantra." At least that wasn't a lie.

"Call her right now to cancel, then text me your location," Jax said. "I'll pick her up too if she gets stuck."

"Jax—"

"The news says the snow's gonna dump two feet," Jax said. "The whole city will be buried."

Meg breathed out, breathed in. Then she cracked. "Okay."

She hung up, and with trembling fingers, she pinned her location, then texted it to Jax.

See you soon, he wrote back.

Her eyes slid shut, and she swallowed against the painful lump in her throat. She hated that she was crying now. She hated that he was helping her tonight. She hated that he'd gone behind her back on the lease.

Meg couldn't feel her toes by the time Jax's truck lights flashed into the parking lot. Relief shot through her at the sight of her rescuer, even though she was reluctant to feel grateful. She'd cancelled the roadside assistance, so she'd call them in the morning to reschedule once the roads had all been plowed.

Meg grabbed her purse and double-checked that the keys and phone were inside, then she climbed out.

"You okay?" Jax said, trudging through the collecting snow toward her car, his gaze scanning her face.

"Fine."

Worry etched his brow. "Wait in the truck. I'll see if I can get it started."

Of course. Typical male. As if she hadn't been sitting in the cold for an hour and hadn't tried a dozen times. "Sure." She handed over her keys, then hurried to the truck through several inches of snow that had fallen. The wind was still fierce, stacking up drifts along the side of the bank building. She hoped that she'd be able to get her car out of the parking lot tomorrow.

Once inside the cab of the truck, Meg gave into the shivering. Her entire body ached with cold. She didn't want Jax to know how desperate she'd been, so by the time he returned from his stubborn check of her car, with no better results, she'd taken several deep breaths to stop her teeth from chattering.

Jax climbed into the truck, and just his large presence, his very maleness, and the way he looked over at her made her stomach clench with regret. Why had he done such a dumb thing? Just when she was letting down her guard and believing that what was going on between them could turn into the real thing.

"It think it's the starter," he said. "How old is the car?"

"Three years."

Jax nodded. "Could be, although it's kind of early for a starter to go out." He eyed her as she stayed close to the passenger door. "Come here; you're shivering."

She was, but she knew any contact with Jax would kill her resolve. "I'm good."

She felt his hesitation, his confusion, but he didn't push her. He pulled out of the parking lot and turned onto the main road. There were flashing lights up ahead—probably an accident—it was as if the entire city had come to a standstill.

Jax took some back roads through neighborhoods she probably normally wouldn't have dared to drive herself, but they were free of accidents.

"Is your grandma okay in this kind of storm?"

"Yeah," Meg said, her voice sounding too high-pitched. "She was at home when it started to snow. She doesn't go out at night by herself anyway."

Jax nodded, then drummed his fingers against the steering wheel. *Tap. Tap. Tap.*

Kind of like her rapid pulse.

She was thawing out, but that only made her emotions surface. Whatever happened, she was determined not to cry in front of Jax. She didn't want his insincere apologies just because she was crying about him giving her money. Someone else might think she was crazy to turn down such a generous offer, but it was the only way Meg could retain her dignity.

TWENTY-THREE

JAX HAD KNOWN something was wrong the minute Meg had answered her phone. She was stressed, that was clear, but it was more than the car breakdown. He wanted to question her about whether it was still under warranty, because the car was creating too much trouble in too short of a time.

But she was on the edge, and he was pretty sure he knew why.

He'd picked her up at the bank . . . and that was clue enough. He let her have her silence on the rest of the drive, though, and as he pulled up to her grandma's, he said, "Meghan, I can explain."

Her inhale was sharp, and he put the truck into park, letting it idle in her grandma's driveway. The snow was nearly a foot deep already, and he was sure he'd be driving to his place with his flashers on. But that didn't matter right now. Making things good with Meg did.

She wiped at her eyes.

Damn.

"Sorry," she said. "I don't mean to cry. I'm mad at myself, in fact, because I cry too much in front of you. But I thought I told you I can't accept your money. I thought you understood. But you've treated it like a joke and disrespected my wishes."

Jax felt like his heart had just been carved out. "Meghan, I don't think it's a joke. I wanted to surprise you, I guess. And hoped that you'd be excited, grateful even."

She turned to look at him, her mascara already smudged.

"Is that what your dad tells you when he donates money to the Flyers? That he hopes you'll be excited? Grateful?"

She couldn't have twisted a knife into his gut any deeper if she'd had a real one.

"Jax, I know you have a good heart," she said with a sniffle. "But this was . . . out of line. And the fact that I have to point it out is broken. It makes me wonder what else might be broken between us. I told myself I'd never date a man who didn't treat me as a person with my own opinions."

Jax wiped a hand down his face. "I didn't mean to make you feel that way."

She was reaching for the door handle, though.

"Wait, Meghan, please, let me explain."

"It's okay," she said. "I can guess what you'll say, and things will be fine for a while. Then something will come up later on, and you'll do the same thing again." The door was open now.

He reached for her arm. "Meg."

"I'm not cut out for this," she said, her voice stronger now. "I can't wait around for you to break my heart twice." She shut the door without giving him a chance to counter her words.

He was out of the truck in a flash. "Meghan, let's talk. Please." He trudged after her, but somehow she was on the porch lightning quick, then inside the house before he reached the first step.

Jax stood on the porch for a long moment. A couple of

lights were on inside the house, but there were no sounds. And he was pretty sure she wouldn't answer if he knocked. Besides, he didn't want to upset her grandma.

He pulled out his phone from his pocket, not even noticing the cold chilling him. *I'm sorry. Please call me.*

He waited several moments on the porch until the cold drove him off, back through the falling snow, and into his truck.

The drive back to his place was slow because of the weather and agonizing because of the pain he'd heard in Meg's tone. He could only hope that she'd call him later. Let him explain. Although what she'd said about him acting like his dad was hitting him in an uncomfortable place.

What had his motivations been? To help out the woman he was falling in love with. Was probably already in love with, if he were to admit it. He didn't want to see her hurt, he didn't want her to have to give up her boutique, he wanted . . . her happy. And if he could be a part of that, then there'd be no question about the money.

Jax groaned.

Like father, like son.

Was it so terrible? To do something extravagant for someone you loved? Even if that person hadn't asked for the help? Hadn't wanted it?

He walked into his house. If someone could be happy tonight, it was Sheriff, so Jax gave him an extra treat. The dog didn't complain. Then Jax went into his office. The photo album was still on the coffee table. The last time he'd been on the couch, Meg had snuggled up to him, and they'd shared some amazing kisses.

Well, everything about her was amazing, and he'd just screwed things up.

He sat on the couch and flipped through a few pages of

the album. The smiling pictures brought back memories. Good memories. Some of which he'd been too much in his selfish head to be grateful for.

Then he called his mom. He was kind of surprised she answered, but she was back in Chicago, and since there was a whiteout storm, he assumed she wasn't at some gala event or dinner party.

"Hi, Mom," Jax said. "I need some advice."

She listened as he poured out the whole story—well, most of it. Some of the more private stuff between him and Meg was edited out, but his mom had not been born yesterday.

When he finished, his mom said, "She was right, son. I'm sorry if that offends you, but she told you no up front, and you went behind her back."

Jax bit back a curse. "Like Dad, is what you're saying."

His mom's sigh was clear. "Your dad's not perfect, and I'll be the first to admit that we don't always see eye to eye. But no, you're not like him, Jackson. You've learned things the hard way, and you have a kind heart. Your dad is still . . . working on that."

"But Meg sees me in the same light."

"Give her some time," his mom said. "I saw the two of you together, and I think you're both made of stronger stuff. This is just a hiccup."

"I hope you're right."

He hung up with his mom, and he could admit he did feel better, but not much. He looked at his messages. Nothing from Meg.

He was done talking. He'd probably say something to Rocco later, since he was the main friend who even knew half of what was going on.

Jax leaned back on the couch, closing his eyes. He wanted to hear her voice. He wanted to see her face. Hold her hand. Beg her for forgiveness. Kiss away her tears.

But twelve hours later, at the airport, there was still no word from Meg. Should he call her grandma? No . . . that would be overdoing it.

"You look like you're going to a funeral," Corbie said, slapping his shoulder before taking a seat next to him in the waiting area near the gate.

Jax shook his head and kept his gaze trained on some downloaded film of the Denver Chargers. He couldn't force Meg to talk to him, so he might as well get ready for the game.

"What's up, man?" Corbie said after a moment, when Jax didn't answer.

"Not much," Jax deadpanned.

"You've already seen those plays," Corbie said. "If you don't want to talk, fine, but I'm here if you need it."

Jax sighed, then shut down his phone. He leaned back in his chair, folded his arms, and stretched out his long legs. "Meg dumped me."

Corbie chuckled, then his eyes widened. "Serious, dude?"

Jax scrubbed at his beard. "Looks like it. Total silence."

"What'd ya do?"

"Screwed up, that's what."

Corbie huffed a breath. "Sorry. That's sucks. Maybe you can send her flowers or something? I mean, I've done that a few times when I'm in a pickle with Jen."

"Maybe."

They sat for a few more minutes in silence as the airport chaos buzzed about them.

"Hey," Jax said. "Does Jen like to shop, you know, for fancy stuff?"

Corbie turned his head to meet Jax's gaze. "Is she a woman?"

Jax smirked. "Can you do me a favor?"

"Anything."

"Tell her about a cool boutique downtown, called Meg's Loft. Tell her to check it out."

Corbie held Jax's gaze for a second, then said, "Okay, consider it done right now." He pulled out his phone and sent a text right then and there.

"Thanks, man."

Twelve more hours later, Jax had scored twice against the Denver Chargers, taken plenty of good-natured crap from the Dice man, and texted Meg three times.

Now, in his hotel room, he was alone again, with plenty of time to think. An email had come in earlier from his bank, telling him that a payment had been refunded to his account. He didn't need to look at the amount to know it was the lease payment.

What was she going to do? Just let it fold? Give up the fight?

He checked the time. One in the morning Chicago time. He wasn't ready to give up any fight. Not if it had to do with Meg. What if he called? Would she answer? Was her phone even on?

He pressed SEND on her number. It rang once, then abruptly shut off.

She'd essentially hung up on him.

Jax groaned and flopped back on his bed. Staring at the ceiling, he sure hoped his mom was right. But he didn't know how he'd survive the wait.

TWENTY-FOUR

"MEG, THERE'S A lady here asking for you," Nashelle said.

Meg looked up from the desk she'd been sitting at in the back room, crunching numbers. The twenty-percent-off sale had done nicely over the past few days, but it was looking like she'd have to start liquidating right after New Year's. And if that went well, she could keep the rest of the stock and convert to online sales.

Nashelle had already been taking pictures for the website. It seemed that she had quite a few talents.

"Can you help her?" Meg asked. She wasn't in the mood to be cheerful with customers who were bargain hunting.

"Um, I think you'll want to speak with this one."

Meg frowned.

"It's *his* mom," Nashelle said in a stage whisper.

Meg didn't need any more clarification. *His* could only mean one person to Nashelle, who'd heard a very shortened and watered-down version of why she wasn't seeing Jax Emerson anymore. It had been three days since she'd seen or spoken to Jax. She'd ignored his texts and calls, although it was probably the hardest thing she'd done in her life. There'd been nothing for about twenty-four hours now, and ironically, that also made her sad.

Meg smoothed back her hair and rose from the desk. "Okay, I'm coming."

Nashelle delivered Meg a triumphant look, then sailed out of the office area. Moments later, Meg followed. Yep. Mrs. Emerson was at the front of the store, looking through a rack of blouses. Meg exhaled carefully and strode toward the woman.

"Hello, Mrs. Emerson," Meg said, keeping her voice casual.

The woman turned, and Meg was struck by some of her features that reminded her of Jax. Meg ignored the ache in her heart.

"Call me Gina," Mrs. Emerson said with a wave of her hand. "This clothing is beautiful."

"Thank you."

Gina picked up one of the blouses from the rack. "Do you have a medium in this?"

"All of our merchandise is on the floor."

Putting back the blouse, Gina picked up another one and checked the size. "Perfect," she murmured.

"Out shopping today?" Meg ventured.

"Actually," Gina said, glancing over at Meg again, "I came to talk to you. But it seems I'm shopping as well."

Meg laughed, although it came out a nervous sound.

"I'll take this one." Gina handed over the blouse.

"Okay, great," Meg said. "Do you want to try it on?"

"No. I'd like to try on that dress, though." She pointed a manicured nail to the silver dress on display. "Please tell me you have my size."

"We do." Meg moved to the rack near the front display and produced a size 8 and held it up.

218

"It's breathtaking," Gina said, grasping the hanger and holding it up.

"Our dressing rooms are in the back."

Gina paused and looked past Meg. Then she refocused on Meg. "Can I ask you something?"

Meg felt heat prickle the back of her neck. "Sure."

"Do you think you could ever forgive my son for what he did?"

Meg's stomach dropped. "Uh, I think that's a very personal question, and one I probably shouldn't be discussing during work hours." She was being pert, and probably rude, but she'd been blindsided.

"I agree that it's personal to you," Gina said in a lowered tone, although Nashelle was out of earshot at the register. "But it's personal to me too. You see, Jax is my son, and he's full of remorse. I've never seen him so dejected, so utterly crushed."

Meg could only stare. Her throat felt like it was being squeezed raw.

"Oh, he won't show it," Gina continued, moving a half step closer. "He wouldn't breathe a word, but a mother knows."

"I—I don't know what to say," Meg finally said, her voice raspy.

"Relationships are complicated, I get it," Gina continued. "More than most people will ever know. And yes, Jax overstepped his bounds. And perhaps it *was* like his father. And yes, the men in my family are the most stubborn men on the planet, but I believe Jax's intentions were pure. He wanted to help the woman he loves, and he didn't think through things clearly enough."

"The woman he loves?" Meg repeated numbly.

Gina smiled—a smile that was more sad than anything. "Jax's in love with you, Meg. I'm not telling you that to make you feel guilty or anything. I'm telling you because my son is a broken man, and only you can fix that."

Meg stepped away. Tears stung her eyes. "What do I do?" she whispered.

"That's up to you, dear," she said. "Although tomorrow night is our annual holiday party at the Palace Hotel. Black tie. It's also Jax's birthday." She held up the cocktail dress and looked at it in one of the wall mirrors. "You're invited, and I hope you'll consider coming."

Meg blinked as Gina moved past her.

"Can I try this on?" Gina said to Nashelle.

Nashelle murmured her assent, but Meg didn't turn around. She was rooted to the floor. *Jax was in love with her?* His mother had come to the shop to invite her to their holiday party? It was Jax's birthday tomorrow?

Her mind churned with questions, doubts, incriminations, but mostly she ached for Jax.

If his pain was even half of her pain, then maybe . . .

"Oh, hi," a young woman said.

Meg hadn't even seen her come into the shop, hadn't even heard the door chime. "I'm going to a party tomorrow night, and I heard you have a fabulous cocktail collection."

"We d-do," Meg said, stuttering over her words. She cast a glance at Nashelle, who shrugged from where she was straightening a rack. "What color are you thinking of?"

"That red one in the window is amazing."

"Great," Meg said.

While the young woman was trying on the red dress, Gina came out of the dressing room. "I'll take it," she said with a smile. "I hope you don't mind, I took a selfie in the dressing room with it on and posted to my Instagram page."

Meg tried not to let her mouth fall open. This woman had an Insta page?

"Thank you," Nashelle said. "What's your Insta? We'll follow you."

While Gina rattled off her Insta profile, Meg tried to breathe normally. She was probably only half coherent when saying goodbye to Jax's mom. She had no time to say anything to Nashelle when the other woman came out of the dressing room.

"I love it," she said. "My boyfriend's going to kill me when he finds out how much this was. But he told me to come here, so it's his fault."

Nashelle smiled. "He'll love it, and he won't even ask how much it cost."

"You don't know Corbie," the woman said. "I mean, he makes good money, but he's still a tightwad." She laughed. "I still love him."

Corbie . . . Meg felt her face drain of color. Corbie was a really unusual name.

"Oh, you're dating the hockey player?" Nashelle said.

The woman's face flushed pink. "Yeah."

"Good for you," Nashelle said. "He can totally afford this dress, and if I were you, I'd get these earrings to go with it."

The woman picked up the earrings and added them to her purchase. She and Nashelle shared a secret smile before the woman waltzed out of the store with her purchases.

"Well," Meg said.

"Well," Nashelle repeated. "Nice chat with Mrs. Emerson?"

"Interesting, to say the least."

Nashelle gave her a coy smile. "I think you should go to the party. I mean, you don't want to miss seeing Jax Emerson in a tux."

"How did you know?"

"Mrs. Emerson was quite chatty."

Before Meg could answer, the shop door opened again, and what looked to be a mother-daughter duo walked in. They, too, bought cocktail dresses, and the mother added another outfit on top of the purchases.

Meg never did return to her laptop, because they were busy the rest of the day. Everyone seemed to need their holiday dresses, and Nashelle had a ball upselling other items along with the dresses.

Going home that night, Meg felt exhilarated. No, she hadn't decided if she'd go to the party the next night, but sales had been fantastic. If only she'd sold like that every day of the month, she wouldn't be closing down. Regardless, it was wonderful to get rid of the inventory, as well as make some ladies very happy with their choices.

Her mind would not shut off, so she took a sleeping pill around midnight, which also meant she overslept. She got to the shop about ten minutes before opening and was shocked to see a group of ladies waiting on the sidewalk for it to open. Meg pulled around to the back parking lot and called Nashelle.

"Can you come in early?" Meg asked in a breathless voice. "We already have customers."

"What? I'm on my way."

Meg hurried to turn on lights and open up the shop. "Sorry to keep you waiting, ladies."

They breezed in, all smiles and chatter, sorting through dresses. They seemed like a close group of friends. By the time Nashelle arrived, Meg had sold four dresses, and three other women had arrived.

Nashelle cheerfully showed ladies to the dressing room and rang up purchases. They had no break that morning, and by the afternoon, Meg was rearranging rounders and bringing out some stock she had already separated out for online orders.

They stayed open thirty minutes past closing time since they couldn't shoo out the women who were lingering over their purchase decisions.

"Oh my gosh," Nashelle said as they finally locked up the place.

"Wow." Meg leaned against the front door. She was exhausted, in a good way.

Nashelle rubbed her hands together. "Did we set a record or what?"

"Definitely." Meg straightened and headed to the register to pull the numbers for the day. Her eyes about popped out when she saw them.

"Holy . . ." Nashelle said, leaning over the counter to look. "That's like four months of sales in one day."

"Yeah." Meg's eyes misted. She laughed, feeling a bit hysterical.

"Did you see the follows on our Instagram account?" Nashelle said suddenly, looking up from her phone.

"No . . ." Meg stared at the number. "Seven hundred and five? How is that possible? We only had a hundred just a few days ago."

Nashelle selected the tags and pulled up pictures from other accounts giving shoutouts to the boutique. "Amazing." She clicked over to Gina Emerson's account, where she'd posted the snapshot of herself in the dressing room in the silver dress, with the caption: *What do you think, ladies? Pretty enough for my son's birthday bash tomorrow? Found it at a hidden gem downtown called Meg's Loft.*

Meg blinked back the burning in her eyes. "She has over a thousand likes and almost a hundred comments."

"Unbelievable," Nashelle said in a reverent tone.

"Let me check something." Meg grabbed her laptop from the back room. She logged into the spreadsheet that downloaded the online sales. There were dozens of new orders. Some things had completely sold out, and as Meg refreshed the spreadsheet, four more orders popped up.

"Meg, this is crazy," Nashelle said. "Do you want me to put in some stock orders?"

Meg met her co-worker's gaze. "What do you think?"

Nashelle's smile widened. "I think yes. We'll put in one overnight order, then we can do more tomorrow if needed."

Meg felt breathless. "Okay. Let's do it." She perched on the stool and started to pull up their order accounts.

"No way," Nashelle said, nudging Meg. "I'm doing the ordering. You're going to grab one of those dresses at the front of the store and go home to get dressed."

"For what?" Meg asked, although her heart was pounding.

Nashelle's smile was coy. "You have a man to wish a happy birthday to."

TWENTY-FIVE

MEG STOOD IN front of the full-length mirror in her bedroom at her grandma's house. She was wearing a black dress with a high neckline, but the sleeves were scooped out, and the back dipped nearly to her waist, exposing her entire back.

It was a daring dress. Sexy but still classy. The skirt flared just above her knees and swirled when she moved. She'd tried on several different pairs of shoes, finally settling on burnished-silver stilettos. It was a bold choice even for her.

A tap sounded on her door, and Meg said, "You can come in, Grandma."

Her grandma entered the bedroom. "You look beautiful."

"Thanks," Meg breathed. But she still felt unsure. Not about the dress or the heels but about seeing Jax. What would she say to him? What would he think when he saw her crash his parents' party and his birthday celebration? Well, she'd technically been invited—but still . . .

Her grandma stepped more fully into the room and turned to look at Meg's reflection in the mirror. "Just remember, you are worth it. And so is he."

Meg released a shaky breath. She'd told her grandma

most of what had happened, and while her grandma agreed that Jax had overstepped his bounds, she was more of the mind of Gina Emerson. This was something that could be worked out. It wasn't a deal breaker.

So Meg was going to put a little more faith into herself, eat some humble pie, and go wish Jax a happy birthday. Come what may.

"It's not too much? Too bare for December?" Meg did a slow turn.

Her grandma only smiled. "It's a dress that will draw attention, there's no doubt. But if you love it, then that's all that matters."

Meg nodded. Nashelle had helped her pick it out, and the earrings of course—silvery dangling ones.

"Go," Grandma said. "Have a wonderful time."

"Thanks," Meg said through a tightened throat. She bent and kissed her grandma's soft cheek.

The night was windless, cold, and clear as she drove to the Palace Hotel. Her nerves wound tighter and tighter with each mile that she grew closer. And then the lights of the hotel sparkled again in the night sky, putting to shame the thousands of winter stars.

She was here. Slowly, she pulled into the valet parking and put her car into park.

Climbing out of her low car, she grasped the door to keep her balance. She thanked the valet, then she walked through the sliding door and followed the lobby signs to the ballroom. It wasn't too hard to find it, with the thumping music practically vibrating the walls.

It was like walking into another world. Holiday lights made the room look like a winter wonderland, and the dance floor was packed. People milled about with glasses of wine. Others were sitting at tables, eating food from the buffet.

Meg hovered near the entrance, scanning for Mrs. Emerson.

When Meg spotted her near the buffet table, speaking to a waiter, she hurried over. She wanted to talk to her before looking for Jax. But her stilettos kept her footsteps careful.

"Meg," Gina said, turning just as Meg reached her.

The air-kiss shouldn't have been a surprise, but it was.

"It's wonderful to see you," Gina continued. "You look beautiful."

"You too," Meg said. "Thank you for posting to Instagram about the store, too."

Gina winked. "No problem. I never shy away from recommending something I like. Now, have you seen Jax yet?"

Before she could answer, Mr. Emerson appeared, his gaze curious.

"You remember Meg Bailey, don't you, dear?" Gina said in a smooth tone.

"I do," Mr. Emerson said, extending his hand.

Then Meg was shaking Jax's father's hand. Nerves danced in her belly.

"I owe you an apology, Miss Bailey," he said. "I jumped to some wrong conclusions about you, but Jax set me straight."

Meg nodded. "He told me."

"Well, then, everything all cleared up?" Mr. Emerson asked, patting her arm. "You going to go dance with our boy and put him out of his misery?"

"Todd," his wife chided. "Meg just arrived. Give her a bit of a break."

"Don't wait too long," he said with a wink at Meg. "He's been brooding too long."

Meg had no words, but Mr. Emerson turned and began talking to someone else in the next moment.

Gina linked her arm through Meg's and drew her away from the two men. "Don't mind him. He's been set down by his son, which I secretly love."

"What happened?" Meg asked, scanning the crowd, not seeing Jax yet.

"Oh, Jax gave him an ultimatum," Gina said. "Told him that he needed to be donating to the Northbrook Elite Hockey Club. Jax wants any contract renewal to come directly from the Flyers. No daddy money involved."

Meg was holding her breath. "And . . . what happened?"

"Todd agreed. You'll have to ask Jax about the rest."

Meg released her breath. "Where is he?"

"Dancing, of course."

Meg's eyes landed on a tall figure toward the center of the dancing floor.

He was dancing with a blond woman. She was gorgeous, and Jax was laughing at something she'd just said. He also looked amazing in a tux, not that Meg had ever doubted.

"I see him." She tried to ignore the stab of disappointment pricking her chest. "He looks happy."

"Yeah, he might look happy, but he misses you, Meg." Gina squeezed her arm. "I probably shouldn't admit this, since Lacy and I became friends, but with Lacy, Jax was . . . always trying to keep up with her demands. It drained him. But with you, he's a better man. You're the other half of his heart."

"So who's the woman he's dancing with?"

Gina smiled. "His cousin. Brenna."

Oh. Okay. The fluttering nerves returned.

The music changed, and Jax led the woman off the dance floor.

"Go to him," Gina said, releasing her arm.

And then Meg was standing on her own, watching Jax join a group of guys. A couple of them clapped him on the back. Their conversation looked lively, jovial, and she was about to walk into the middle of it.

She forced one step in front of the other, keeping her eyes on Jax while at the same time willing herself not to trip. She shouldn't have worn the stilettos. She wouldn't be surprised if she twisted an ankle, because at that moment, she reached the circle, and six pairs of eyes looked at her.

Jax turned as well, since everyone in his group had stopped talking when they spotted her.

"Hi, Jax," she said the moment their eyes connected.

She needed no introduction to this group. She'd met them all—Rocco, Bones, Corbie, Clint, and Lucas.

Jax hadn't budged. Even in the dim lighting, she felt his eyes on her, moving from her face down to her shoes, then back up again. His shoulders seemed broader somehow, and his beard was shorter, but everything else was the same. His eyes, the slope of his nose, those lips she'd tasted many times.

She kept moving toward him, although she was pretty sure her legs were trembling, and she definitely couldn't catch a full breath. Six pro athletes were about to watch her grovel. When she stopped in front of Jax, somehow the music faded.

In the multicolored lighting, his eyes were nearly black, and at this moment she sure hoped his mom had been right. That he'd take her back in a heartbeat, that he didn't hate her but instead . . . loved her.

And she sure hoped he was in the mood for forgiveness.

"Meghan, what are you doing here?" he asked.

His low tones felt like a surge of warm water had washed over her. It had been too long since she'd heard his voice. Listening to his old messages didn't count. "I came to wish you a happy birthday."

No expression. No reaction.

Behind her, one of his friends said something about

getting another drink at a bar. Another mentioned he was going to hit the buffet. One said he'd spotted an old friend; another needed some cold air. Rocco murmured something about collecting on a bet. And then they were truly alone—or as alone as they could be in a ballroom full of people.

Meg exhaled and bravely held his gaze. "Do you want to dance?"

"Meghan—"

"And don't tell me you can't dance," she said in a rush, since she was pretty sure he was about to turn her down, and that would ruin all her plans, "because I saw you dancing with your cousin, and you were excellent."

He rubbed his neck, his gaze dropping. "You can't just show up here, Meghan, wearing a dress like that," he said in a low voice only she could hear, his eyes perusing her again slowly enough that goosebumps pricked her arms, "and ask a man to dance without him wondering what's going on."

Another exhale. So maybe he'd take a bit of cajoling. "A lot of things have happened, Jax, but one is the most important. Which is why I swallowed my stupid pride and took your mom's advice and—"

"Wait, you talked to my mom?"

Meg nodded. "I don't know if I can answer all of your questions, but I do want to apologize."

"For what?"

His mom was right. He was the most stubborn man on the planet.

"For ghosting you. For not calling you back. For not listening to you when you needed me to. For not telling you how I feel. For not . . . trusting you."

His eyes narrowed. "That's a lot of apologizing."

"There's more."

"Maybe we should dance, then," he said. "I think we have an audience."

She glanced around to see that indeed, there were a lot of curious onlookers trying not to look curious. But Meg wasn't fooled. Before she could comment, Jax grasped her hand and led her into the heart of the dance floor.

She almost sagged at his touch, but she didn't. Biting her lip, she kept her head lifted, her heart contained in her chest.

And they danced. Just like that. Not a word between them as Jax took the lead. He really was a good dancer. Had his mom made him take dance lessons, or was it something he'd done with a girlfriend? However he'd learned, her mind soon turned to the fact that she was dancing with Jax. His hands were on her, drawing her close, his clothing brushing against hers, and his familiar scent made memories rush back. All of which she'd never forgotten.

The music shifted to a much slower number, and Meg thought she caught a glimpse of Rocco leaving the DJ stand. Had he requested something?

But it was like Jax had been waiting for the slower song, because he drew her closer with no hesitation. His large hand pressed against the bare skin of her lower back. He stalled for a moment, as if just realizing how low-cut the back of her dress was. Then he pulled her close as his other hand engulfed her hand. He lowered his head so that she could feel the tickle of his beard against her cheek. "What did my mom tell you?" his voice rumbled next to her ear.

Meg closed her eyes, breathing in his familiar spicy, clean scent as goosebumps raced over her skin. Her heart literally ached with how much she'd missed him. "She said that you were really grumpy."

He chuckled, and the vibration made her heart skip a beat. "That's true."

"And she said that you missed me."

He hesitated, then said, "That's true too." His voice was lower, softer.

A thrill ran through her, and she moved her hand higher up on his shoulder so that her fingers could brush the back of his warm neck.

"She also told me that you're in love with me. Or you were," Meg said next to his ear. "I don't know if she was right, but . . ." Her heart was racing so much that she was having trouble catching a full breath, but she had to finish. "But I love *you*, Jax Emerson, and I'm sorry I was too caught up in my self-righteousness to admit it."

There. She was out of breath, but she'd told him.

His hand moved up her back, creating a path of fire as his palm trailed along her bare skin. "Say it again," he whispered.

She bit her lip, then said, "I love you." She felt his smile against her neck. And then he pressed a kiss against her jaw.

"That's good to hear, Meghan Bailey," he murmured, then he kissed her below her earlobe.

"Jax," she breathed. "Does this mean you accept my apologies?" Although she was pretty sure he did.

He lifted his head, and this time she could read his gray eyes. And they said *yes*.

"Have you confessed all of them?" His gaze dipped to her mouth.

She smiled. "I think so."

"Then the answer is yes." He leaned his forehead against hers. "And I still love you, Meghan. My feelings aren't in the past, not by a long shot."

She couldn't stop the grin spreading on her face.

Jax released her hand and ran his thumb along her jaw, both hands cradling her face as he continued to sway her with the music. Then he kissed her, on the mouth. And it wasn't a brief kiss. His hand inched behind her neck, and his other hand slid over her shoulder to the middle of her back as he anchored her against him.

When he let her breathe again, she whispered, "Everyone's watching."

"I don't care," he rumbled, then he kissed her again.

Meg slid her arms about his neck. In for a penny, in for a pound. She was pretty sure she heard some clapping going on. And an "It's about time" that sounded suspiciously like Rocco's voice.

The delicious kiss came to a slow end, but Jax was nowhere close to putting any space between them. "I know you've turned me down, multiple times, but my investment offer still stands."

"Here's the thing, Jax," Meg said, tracing the edge of his collar with her fingers. "I called my landlord tonight with the news that I want to extend at least another month. Yesterday and today we had record sales. Nashelle is ordering more stock to be overnighted."

"That's great." Jax didn't look at all surprised, which only confirmed her suspicions.

Meg smiled. "I think I have a little bird to thank for putting the word out. Two birds. You and your mom."

"Hmm." Jax gazed at her. "I like seeing you happy."

"*You* make me happy."

"I like that even better."

She looped both arms around his neck and pulled him closer, no longer caring who was watching or talking about them. "Your mom said that you gave your dad the ultimatum."

Jax's mouth quirked. "You two are pretty tight, huh?"

"It's all new."

Jax chuckled, and one of his hands settled at her waist. "My dad's putting his money into the Northbrook club. And we'll see what happens with Coach Lindon, how much he wants me on the Flyers."

Not exactly what Meg was hoping for, but it was a beginning, and she could see the harmony in Jax's eyes.

She brushed the edges of his hair. "What are you hoping for?"

"Whatever's best for us."

"Us?"

His eyes didn't leave her face. "I want you coming with me, Meghan. Wherever I go, whatever happens. If it's Chicago, then that's fine. If it's another city, then you can open up a chain of boutiques."

Jax was being kind of presumptuous, but her heart was expanding, and she knew, without a doubt, that she belonged with this man.

"I won't force you, of course," he said, lowering his face to hers. "But I will try my best to convince you."

Meg released a shaky breath, then smiled. "I'm familiar with your tactics."

He grinned. "I love you, Meghan Bailey."

"And I love you, Jax Emerson," she whispered. "And don't worry, I'm already convinced. Wherever you go, I'll come too."

He scooped her close and lifted her off the ground.

She squealed, and Jax laughed. Then he kissed her, not holding back a thing. People around them started clapping. Meg was sure she was bright red with the attention, but she was in Jax's arms, Jax's world, and she didn't want to be anywhere else. Ever again.

Heather B. Moore is a four-time *USA Today* bestselling author. She writes historical thrillers under the pen name H.B. Moore; her latest thrillers include *The Killing Curse* and *Breaking Jess*. Under the name Heather B. Moore, she writes romance and women's fiction. Her newest releases include the historical romances *Love is Come* and *Ruth*. She's also one of the coauthors of the *USA Today* bestselling series: A Timeless Romance Anthology. Heather writes speculative fiction under the pen name Jane Redd; releases include the Solstice series and *Mistress Grim*. Heather is represented by Dystel, Goderich & Bourret.

For book updates, sign up for Heather's email list: hbmoore.com/contact
    Website: HBMoore.com
    Facebook: Fans of H. B. Moore
    Blog: MyWritersLair.blogspot.com
    Instagram: @authorhbmoore
    Twitter: @HeatherBMoore